Chrono

Vault

Mars

As humanity sets out on a renewed course to the stars,
this extraordinary tale explores the possibilities of what we
might discover when first we set foot on another planet.
Secret documents hidden in a lava tube on Mars for thousands
of years reveal a tale so astonishing and timely in its subject
matter that it could overthrow the minds of some
and be the salvation of others.

Books in the following series:
Reign of the Dragon

A New Star Ascends
War of the Shadows
Thor's Valour
The Thunder God Arises
Valhalla's Hammer
Dragon Fire and Destruction
Quest for Dragons
Veil of Evil
The Ice Warrior War
Conquest of the Stars
Peace of the Hammer
The Glory of Power
Bridge Over Time
A Guide to Arya

Author's Note

Chrono Vault Mars is a work of fiction. All ideas, statements and events are simply there to form part of a structure to entertain and broaden the mind.

Table of Contents

Intro

I cannot tell you exactly how I came by the secret time vault documents so I'm going to give you an alternate fictional account of what happened. If I broke some rules and took some risks I can only say that I consider myself blameless, especially given how much of importance is at stake.

The crux of the matter is that it seems we did not originate on Earth but on a planet far away in this galaxy — so far away that nothing short of the most astonishing events could have delivered us here — twenty thousand light years from our original home and effectively in another universe.

Our ancient Aryan forebears, including the great ruler, Thor, apparently the very same Thor of ancient Norse mythology, appear to have enjoyed considerable intelligence and understood the challenges we might face. In their wisdom, they left us key insights from another time and took thorough measures to ensure that they would not be lost.

So far away this world of Arya is and the time of these histories so long ago that we have to be grateful the gods took such special measures. In storing the data, they used two basic forms. One was simple text inscribed on enduring gold sheets and the other was an advanced digital data module. They recorded stories for posterity then hid them in a vault deep in a lava tube on the dead planet of Mars, in a place where we could find them only once we had become technically advanced enough either to destroy ourselves or venture into space.

As with so many challenges, breakthrough only comes when you are about to break.

As I cannot tell you how I got access to these histories, I have created a fictional account of how they were discovered in the future, which is this tale, Chrono Vault Mars.

The planet Arya is a pivotal element of the understanding Thor gave us. It seems it was different to Earth in various ways both subtle and obvious, leading to its sentient inhabitants developing mentally in directions we do not fully understand.

This resilient mental integrity, in the face of dire challenges, led the Aryans to discover great powers that would make them seem, to lesser beings, like gods. They travelled to Earth, which they called Midgard, settled it and lived here for many thousands of years before eventually moving on.

The Mars vault also contained a further set of six stories in our own prehistory, The Rings of Fate, that occurred many thousands of years after the Aryans came here yet still thousands of years in our past.

The first set of stories is relevant to us because it informs us about Aryan history, namely key events and strong moral challenges at the time of the greatest threat to their existence — not dissimilar to the sorts of challenges we currently face.

The second set of stories was relevant for different reasons. It told of remarkable events that if true, must have occurred on this world more than seven thousand years in our past.

These stories of a noble culture in our past hold great potential to heal us emotionally when our capacity to own honour and justice at its weakest, understandable as that is in the early phases of a technological age.

Thus, Chrono Vault Mars, a story of fortune, love, political intrigue, espionage and rebellion, is the only legally expedient way that I can introduce to you these nineteen tales that stretch back over twenty thousand years into our past.

My own addition to the collection are the six stories of the Little River Rebellion which show the need for the strongest of action at this time in dealing with the current issues of grievous degradation in our world.

Together, the three connected series, The Reign of the Dragon, The Rings of Fate and The Little River Rebellion, offer unique yet connected perspectives on three very different eras of humanity.

You are about to embark on a saga of matchless reach and scope with stalwart values that have enormous potential to restore our collective capacity for hope, courage, conscience and rapture.

Chapter 1 — Evil Chance

The hot coffee steamed in Sarah's hand, warming her, and the burger smelt good. Early September in Florida, 2045, was unseasonably cold and wet, and she was tired. Stepping out into the wind and rain had been unpleasant but she would be back in the car in moments.

The work vehicle was a heavy SUV — white, plain and boring but secure. It made her feel safe, especially when security was tailing her home, but right now they seemed to have disappeared. She had stopped short of Titusville to kill two birds with one stone — wait for her minders and get something to eat.

She clicked the remote only feet away from the vehicle but just as she pulled the door open and slid into her seat a slight bump on the rear of her seat made her freeze.

'That's right, honey, you've got company. Gotcha hot coffee and a liddle present too. No, don't move. Got you covered.'

He moved a little closer to her.

'Just get comfy now an y'll be alright.'

Something made Sarah's heart sink like a stone in a cold lake — something that wanted to make you afraid and wouldn't let go. Where the hell was the security tail?

'What do you want?'

Something pressed hard into her back near her right kidney. She contemplated screaming but no one else was around.

'Dunno. What you got?'

'You want a lift somewhere?' she asked nervously, getting in.

Damn it, why had she stopped for coffee? She could have waited.

'I'll gi you a lift, baby,' came the cold purr from the back seat.

'Really ... you're going to rape me?'

That was met with silence for a few moments.

'Sno' what I'm here for. How much money you got? Wa's in that case?'

'Not money.'

'Well, why don't you show me now?'

'It's only documents. Nothing that could possibly interest you.'

A firm hand gripped her around the throat from behind.

'So, I'm just a dufus, right? Wouldn't understand ... sthat it?'

Sarah's heart stilled again then pounded hard.

'I didn't mean ... it's just that you couldn't get any money from them. They're not worth anything.'

'Mighty fancy case fo' somethin' not worth anything. Drive an don't slow down. You'll tract 'tention to us ... an you reach for anything, yo' gone.'

She started the engine and reversed out slowly. It was all far too strange. The security detail's vehicle must have broken down but why hadn't they called her? The phone was in its cradle. She accelerated out onto the road.

'Have you ... have you got a gun?'

That was her emergency phrase to wake up the phone and send an auto alert but the little red light failed to switch on.

'Got one ... but don't need one.'

'I do have some money in my wallet ... and there's some in the glove box.'

'Oh no, don't you go pokin around in there. More 'n likely got a piece I reckon. Head up the next side road an we'll take us a look.'

Soon Sarah made a left turn and not long after pulled over beneath some trees.

'Okay, slow now ... slow an steady.'

She reached for the glove box and popped it open.

'Wait!' he barked and for the first time Sarah risked a backward glance. He was dressed in black and had a balaclava, covered from head to toe. 'Head between yer knees and hands behind yer back.'

The man reached over and pulled out the standard issue pistol, then the small roll of money.

'Couple a hunnerd here, bitch. Think I'm gunna fall fer that?'

'I don't know. I don't know what you want.'

'Wanna be rich, bitch. Open that case.'

She shivered.

'I can't. I'd lose my job ... maybe more.'

'So, it is important.'

'Not to you.'

'Don't care, open it.'

'I can't. You'll just have to shoot me.'

There was silence for a few terrible seconds.

'Not afraid, huh. We'll jus take a drive to the beach then. Up ninety-five then off to Port Orange then down to Ponce an' the wall.'

Sarah was going to protest the distance but then thought better of it. It might give her more time to come up with something.

'Okay, but I don't see what difference it will make.'

'Just do it. I got me some friends near there.'

Sarah drove in silence, not too fast on her captor's instructions. Nothing happened on the way there but she failed to come up with any sort of escape plane. When they reached the Lighthouse Point carpark, it was empty and the wind had begun to howl even stronger than before. Spray flew up from the end of the breakwater where the waves were pounding on it with increasing ferocity.

'Get out and take the bag with you.'

'Where are we going?'

'For a walk.'

'You are going to rape me.'

'Mebbe.'

'Then I'm not getting out.'

He reached over and grabbed an arm, twisting it behind her back. It hurt and then it hurt more. She screamed.

'Shut up!'

'I will if you stop hurting me.'

He eased his grip but before she could do anything he was hauling her out through the front door. He grabbed the bag and thrust it into her arms then held her tightly by the top of her left arm, dragging her towards the breakwater.

'Why are we going up there?' she asked. 'In this storm, it could be really dangerous.'

'Dangerous for you.'

'For both of us. You ever been here in a storm before?'

'Course, yer jus a pussy. I'll be alright, but if you don't open that case I'm gonna throw you in.'

Just then there was a flash of lightning not far off the end of the breakwater and an almost immediate clap of thunder. The spray was flying thick and fast, almost horizontal.

Sarah resisted as much as she could but her captor was a big man and he half dragged half pushed her up onto the walkway with brutal determination.

On the wall the wind was screaming and she felt like she was being pushed into a hurricane but her captor was strong and he forced her onwards. About halfway along the walkway part, there was more lightning and a series of huge waves hit the end of the wall making it shudder under their feet. Wet spray hit their faces but the man dressed all in black pressed on.

'You wanna go in there, bitch?'

'Nooo,' she cried back, struggling vainly.

'Then open the damn case.'

'I can't. I told you that. It's too important and my security detail travels separately with the key.'

He laughed, whether at the incompetence of her security or the admission of the clear value of the case she couldn't tell.

'Then it's gotta be worth somethin, don't it?'

Sarah yelled in suppressed rage.

'To everyone, maybe, but not to just one person.'

'You a scientist then?'

She paused.

'No, I'm a translator.'

'Spy stuff?'

'No, not exactly.'

The black clad figure stiffened. It smelled like bullshit. She was bullshitting him. He dragged her again for a minute or two, closer to the end of the wall. Another big wave hit and the wall shuddered. A sheet of spray whipped them and all of a sudden Sarah felt like she was freezing. More lightning came in several bursts close together and she saw several huge waves building off the end of the breakwater wall. That was a long way out past the end of the walk but they were huge. She struggled but he would not let go.

'Alright, I work for NASA and when my security detail finds me, you're finished. My work is important ... very important.'

'So, you is a spy!'

'No, you fool, I'm a translator, like I said. It's stuff they found off-world and I'm the chief analyst. It's old, really old and it's amazing. It has the potential to transform our world but it's not about money. You're going to ruin it all ... for everybody.'

The wave hit and the wall groaned. Both of them saw immediately that it was much larger than any before. It loomed like a mountain to the north-east of the wall and even the spray just ahead of it slapped them down onto the rocks. When the main force of the water hit, Sarah was carried over the side into the Ponce Inlet, winded but conscious, the case with her. The figure clad all in black was taken the opposite way, out into the pounding thunderous surf off the beach, wrenched and rolled a dozen times along the sandy bottom until all sign of breath or life was gone.

Morning came, bright and clear, washed clean by tearing wind and torrential rain. A few brave souls trod the sodden sand in the clear morning light but none dared come close to the still raging sea.

Alexander Jamieson, Alex to his friends, was in good spirits. After a long career in TV news and current affairs, not solely built on his rugged good looks, sandy hair and six-foot frame, his uptight wife had divorced him and taken almost everything worth having — but now in the wake of all that he was free.

Heir to his uncle's modest fortune, he had three million in cash and the property when sold would net another two. Liz was not going to get a single iota. He had settled much of it in crypto and she would never know — nor would the government, which would otherwise divvy it all up as it saw fair.

The very idea of a government machine having any concept of fair made him laugh, which he was doing all too often now.

Iota was discreet, fair, reliable, fast and accessible throughout the whole world and it made his heart warm. Waves thundered onto the beach still and their noise and thunderous pulse made him realize that he had strayed a little too close.

A rush of cool water surged around his knees then something hard bumped against his lower leg. A hard case — charcoal grey, a little large than a briefcase, he saw as he bent down to pick it up. One side had been stoving in, smashed hard against the rocks of the breakwater nearby no doubt.

Alex moved back away from the reach of the surf with the case in his hands, wondering if it was empty. It felt like it, apart from maybe some water and sand. It was plastic but the tough kind. The blow that had broken through it must have been heavy. It was not easy pulling back the triangular shaped flap but eventually he managed to and let the water pour out.

Feeling around inside amongst the residual sand and water, he came across a small, hard object and pulled it out. About an inch and a half long, barrel shaped and made of cast aluminium, one end looked as if it could be unscrewed. Yes, it turned. It was a cap and when he removed it he saw that the object was a flash USB drive — and a quality one. He replaced the cap and put it in his shirt pocket before continuing his walk.

Alex left the broken case, noting that the locks, still in place and unopened, seemed secure and strong, and strode up the dune towards the carpark.

On the way back, a pretty brunette flashed a brilliant smile at him — on the way down to the beach for a walk, herself. He returned the smile but kept walking. Farther down to the south a number of people had gathered and there was some sort of commotion, but it was quite a distance away and he was out of time.

Later, he found himself caught up in a frenzy of pre-departure activity, scarcely having time even to glance in the mirror and pat down his unruly hair.

In the end, there was a delay getting a taxi and he made it to the airport only just in time.

After an uneventful check-in, he settled into his business class seat, eased the seatback down and only as he began to relax, the USB drive popped back into his brain.

Slapping his right hand onto his chest, he was relieved to feel it still there in his pocket and set about extracting his laptop from the carry bag.

Chapter 2 — Opportunity

The damn drive was encrypted. Of course it was. Nothing was ever that easy but hell, what did it matter? Things were running his way. Uncle James had been a career cryptologist and while Alex had not exactly shared his interest, there were times when he had assisted in research and he had a rough basic knowledge of what he knew. He had also saved all Uncle James's work onto his computer before leaving and there might be something in all that which would help.

Alex scanned though his uncle's folders and could not see anything likely but then one caught his eye. Breaker Morant? Uncle James was a booklover of the old order. He despised e-books. Why would he have one — just one, on his computer?

One click and he knew that he was on the right track. The screen glowed blue and a button appeared with the word 'initiate' on it. He clicked that then a field appeared with buttons to select either a file or a drive. He clicked the drive one and buttons appeared for each drive including the USB. He clicked on the USB and the program began to run. In less than a minute, the program stopped and the USB drive opened.

A single folder name appeared:

Time Vault of the Gods.

Inside the folder there were sixteen files. Nine novel-like titles had been translated. Five more had not yet been translated and were in a strange language and script unlike anything he had ever seen. There was another file in English that appeared to be an appraisal with chapter headings included such things as Source, Linguistic Features, Cultural Elements, Intent and Moral Integrity. Yet another was a sort of symbolic alphabet that seemed to have been left to enable any finder to translate the original script.

The jet went through a patch of turbulence and Alex had to close the laptop for a while — but he could not wait to open it again and continue reading. The first chapter titled Source spoke of material that had been recovered from a lava tube.

That was remarkable enough but when the technical details revealed that the material had been recovered by a robot in a no-oxygen environment, he knew that the title, Time Vault of the Gods, was not simply for effect. Where could it have been? Mars? The Moon?

The whole thing could be a hoax or an elaborate fiction but the case in which the USB drive was held had been a strong, expensive one and the locks of a well-engineered kind.

So, what was the rest of the material? Was it what had been recovered or was it unrelated? If it was the recovered text, why on Earth were there all these fiction style titles? If the gods had left information for humanity, wouldn't they have left scientific knowledge?

And were these files translations from the strange unidentifiable script? The file sizes equated. The nine translated files and five untranslated, if they were that, matched the largest untranslated one.

The first translated file, A New Star Ascends, was the first of a series titled Reign of the Dragon. Alex read a few pages and found that it had a normal enough style. It just seemed like some contemporary story but it seemed to be about another world and the principal character was a twelve-year-old *boy* called Thor.

Thor? A twelve-year-old boy?

It all seemed so unlikely for something that had been found on Mars and hidden perhaps for thousands of years. The intro made mention of an Arya star, which could be anywhere — but the first chapter focused on a series of adversities experienced by the boy, Thor. The lad seemed quite human in every sense of the word. Alex got the sense of things fairly quickly that this story might be some sort of background — the early beginnings of a much larger tale.

The second title was War of the Shadows. The first few pages of this title read like an abbreviated history but beyond that, it developed as a relatively conventional sort of thriller. It dealt with Thor now as a young man who strove and dreamed and fought wrongdoing very much like a strong, capable Earth man.

There were hints of ancient ambience in the tale yet Thor had tech. He owned and drove what was obviously a sophisticated internal combustion powered vehicle in a city clearly designed to accommodate such things. It also spoke of secrecy and rebellion against cruel tyranny. For Alex, after many years of independent journalism, this was indeed grist for the mill.

While he read on, hostesses came and went several times, conveniently leaving drinks and snacks without a word. What he was reading about was another world, by name but it was clearly nothing like Mars. There were druids and telepaths and a cultural philosophy known as The Mindcraft Code. Many things seemed familiar and made sense while others did not. The enemy was The Meccanat and it was their government. Alex laughed. How apposite! And yet how ingenuous?

It could be real.

So far, this Arya place might be Earth for all he knew, as portrayed in some strange culture, but what white culture, and this was clearly a white man with golden hair and blue eyes, had such a strange language or script? There were no druids to speak of in today's world and no acknowledged telepaths. If Mars had ever had such a civilization it was completely obliterated now. In which case, if this material was somehow real, what was the point of the story?

Dinner came, and he quickly saved the files to the internal drive. He packed the tough little USB drive away carefully.

After dinner, he began to read again from 'Wrath of the Thunder God', and now there was something that proved this tale was not about Earth or even Mars. For one thing, the planet had two moons. There it was in black and white, so to speak:

"In truth, these hidden paths were a palpable danger, largely unlit as they were — at least until Vilyas, the first to rise of the two Aryan moons, bathed the land in his comforting golden glow and a little light descended through the great forest of towers."

Some of the words were strange, even in translated form, like sashay, which clearly meant a larger car or sedan, but which implied swagger or style. Whoever had translated this work had done so with creditable care and sympathy. Also, Aryans strangely referred to their sun as the star or the Arya star.

Thor's closest female assistant, Eirein, had violet eyes and luxuriant blond hair. The only people on Earth who had such features were northern European or of such extraction, yet none had truly violet eyes and none that Alex knew of were quite like these people.

Finishing the first chapter, he found a footnote. Good god! The first date was 437 in Meccanat Rule reckoning but it was 99955 in the alternative 'Keisari Rule' reckoning. That was 45 years shy of 100,000 years of presumably recorded history. And what a strange co-incidence that the recently deposed rulers of Arya were called Keisari — the Norse word for a ruler.

Why were the names of their rulers the same as many of Earth's? Keisari was Scandinavian and came from Caesar and so too did Kaiser and Tzar. Alex felt pale all of a sudden then began to sweat.

The thought of such an ancient and sophisticated culture having existed at some time in the long distant past was stirring, more exciting than anything he had encountered in years but it was also a little unnerving, given that this was clearly so secret.

The arrow thought of these Aryans, as they called it, was a clear and precise form of communication. It was far more than simply a telepathic feeling or impression. Alex wondered if humanity had ever had such a capacity. The writer had mentioned the druids and the spirits and the people of their world seemed far more in touch with its natural aspects. Was this what gave them telepathic abilities or was it something less mysterious?

As they flew west into the slowly deepening night, Alex continued to read enthusiastically and found that this character, Thor, remained throughout many years the secret leader of the rebel group he had started — the Shadow Circles.

The fifth chapter featured strange bird-like creatures called krite with poisonous razor-sharp beaks that were clearly not found on Earth. More importantly, this new chapter clarified the purpose and sense of responsibility of the rebel group, not to mention why there was such a desperate need for it on Arya.

Whatever influence had been unleashed on this previously idyllic society was clearly set upon alienating people, tearing the culture apart and wrecking their fundamental relationship with the land.

As leader of this group called the Shadow Circles, Thor had a powerful alter ego: Wraith, or in certain other circumstances, the Shadow Avenger. In one sense, the story and its characters were instilled with many comic book hero attributes but the circumstances of these people were truly dire and the highly embroidered heroism was actually a worthy response to it.

Something strange was behind what had happened to this society and things had come to such a pass that courage needed to be actively understood in the face of the cold, brooding and debilitating fear. That much felt familiar and Alex admired it, reacting to the conscious heroism with appreciation.

Reading on, he noted that the much-feared Ice Warriors were mentioned, mythical beings though they seemed to be on that world. Surely this world of Arya could not be the true source of the ancient myths of the Norse gods? In truth, how could this even be about gods if their world had been invaded and secretly controlled by a corrupt alien force? Yet, if that was the case, could it not also be so here on Earth, where everyday life had reached such a low ebb?

With night deepening, the lights were turned down low and Alex had much to think about. He stretched out and before long slept, dreaming of a distant world with two moons and a secret evil pervading its night. Tall men in bright armour battled shadowy figures with long swords and huge golden dragons hurling vast boulders into tall towers of obsidian.

Before long the epic action of the dream faded away and he felt now that he was the child Thor growing up in a beautiful home — a castle in fact with many fine, tall towers in a valley surrounded by snow-capped mountains.

As the dream progressed, Alex became more and more absorbed in this new experience and began to feel it as if it was his own life.

Thor was bright, happy and well-loved but one night when he lay down to sleep, a dark shadow crept in through the window, high above the ground though it was, and laid poisonous hands upon him.

As he lay there, he felt something cold, dark and withering spread through him and then he began to fall, shooting down forwards through some endless blackness. Air rushed past him with an increasingly loud roar and the cold was searing and bitter. Horror grew within him as he wondered where and how that fall would end but then came a sudden and unexpected transition into a strange and ghastly scene.

Staring at the appalling tableau before him, he first felt shock then fierce and bright anger. A slow secondary wave of disgust engulfed him then as he witnessed the writhing and shuddering of a man shackled cruelly to a stone wall. The wretched figure moaned pitifully and red welts stood forth on his stomach and legs along with a cold sweat on his pinched face. Faint glimmers of light from torches on the walls flickered and flared occasionally, revealing the place as some sort of primitive dungeon — but then it faded and he emerged again into a new scene, equally horrifying.

High up on a cliff near a great waterfall, a boy stood in fear and loathing, facing a large silvery black serpent that stood raised on its coils before him no more then a few yards away.

Meeting his gaze intently, the serpent's dark eyes seemed to pierce right through his and he felt as if life and hope were rapidly withering away.

Trembling at first in a rough, grinding sort of way — half anger and half fear, he was then gripped by a powerful urge to turn and run yet in that moment, the energy within him changed, beginning to lift him instead, the vibrations of fear within him accelerating until they were something else entirely — a blinding white blur of pure energy.

Instead of turning and falling over into the oblivion of the deep precipice behind him, he exerted great effort from a deep and mysterious place, standing back now even from the blaze of wild energy.

It was clear this serpent was no mindless, purposeless animal but a being with some quality of hidden power. It was quite beautiful in a way, charcoal silvery black and adorned with sweeping lines of bronze extending back from just above its deep indigo eyes.

Alex felt the trial as surely as this twelve-year-old boy Thor might have done and he felt courage return in sympathy with him. Only then did he begin to return to some sort of objective awareness of himself as distinct from the young boy in the vision.

This realization gave him new courage and the final echoes of the rough waves of emotion that had gripped him softened and melted away like a morning frost.

Then, in bare moments, right before him was a tall and beautiful lady standing in a swirling golden aura. She smiled down upon him then raised her right hand towards the sky. Alex was now just enough aware of himself and his own existence to hear the boy's thoughts as something outside of himself.

Young Thor asked her where she had come from but before the words could take shape, he became aware that he could see right through her. She had colour and form in every way and her eyes moved sensibly as she observed his reactions but, astonishingly, there were shiny rocks in the pool below the waterfall visible directly behind her.

Her face softened and her expression saddened to witness the surprise and alarm that her insubstantial ethereal form had triggered. Alex felt the tension ease a little in sympathy with Thor as she lowered her gaze and turned her head slightly to one side. Then she raised her eyes again and looked deep into his.

There was then a flooding return of a sense of peace and beauty along with a strong aura of power and liberation.

'Who are you?' Thor asked.

'That I cannot tell you,' she replied after a while with a languid smile, as the vision faded.

The angelic presence within grew, however, and filtered through into Alex's awareness through Thor's deeply stressed mind like an ocean of love.

Truly, there was more in this world than the cruel shadow of evil.

A fizzing reverberating sensation passed through Alex and the peace was gone, replaced with a torrential cascade of rippling new energy.

Then he was back on Earth but somehow not in his seat on the jet — nor was he indeed awake yet. He knew instantly where he was — a place he both feared and loved by many — the high waterfall at Wentworth Falls in the Blue Mountains west of Sydney.

Around him, the world sang with vibrancy and beauty. The sun shone bright and there was a swift breeze from the west carrying puffy white clouds as well as a light veil of spray from the magnificent waterfall that thundered below him.

Surprisingly, when he turned to face the valley, there was another beautiful vision before him in this his near favourite place in the world, a girl, younger than the great lady before, smiling and carefree but the moment he saw and recognized her he knew what was happening. He had not only seen it but experienced it all before. His heart raced as her eyes connected with his and he froze. She stood there just yards from him, camera in hand, outside the safety fence on the slippery shining rock just above the seven-hundred-foot fall.

One moment she was smiling at him, then she slipped and fell to her knees, sliding back a couple of feet. What could he do? Even as before he was frozen and it felt strangely like the present. Again, she began to slide, cruelly, inevitably.

'Drop the damn camera, Cara!' he called out. 'Lie down flat and dig in with your finger nails!'

He sprang over the fence then launched himself hard across the mossy rock surface of the river, crucially a little above her so that he could safely reach the other side. Just below where Cara was now, there was a slight dip. Once she was there, she would slide again faster and there would be no stopping her — but a largish sapling grew on the edge just above it.

Sheer speed carried him safely over the glistening slippery rock surface and he pulled himself up onto the grassy bank on the other side. Cara was alternately moaning and calling out to him in raw panic now but at least she *was* lying flat and trying to dig in.

Heart pounding harder now, he scrambled over to the sapling at the edge and he held it. It didn't look very strong at the base with the roots in a lump of soil that had all but been washed away in the last big rains — but it was the only way. The young eucalypt bent over under his weight as he slipped down again onto the bare rock surface. Just as he did so, Cara lost the scant grip she had on the muddy, greasy rock.

She was sliding towards him fast. It looked like she might come within reach but what could he grab hold of? Would she reach out to him?

She was screaming and his heart beat mercilessly on the inside of his chest, faster and faster. Alex caught her fingers as she came within reach and slowed her but they were slipping through his grasp. He thrust himself out a little farther to make a lunge for her long golden hair then felt, through his left hand, the sapling roots begin to crack.

He got a good hold on her hair and she stopped but if the sapling's roots broke, they would both be gone.

Lying on his left side with his right foot wedged under a small rocky outcrop on the bank to ease the stress on the sapling, he pulled himself back with his stomach muscles so that he could move his other hand farther up the now horizontal sapling trunk, striving to reach for the tangle of old roots at its base before pulling harder to get her up out of the dip. In the end, his fingers found something stronger and he started to pull her up.

She was crying out again, probably in pain from having a clump of her hair pulled so hard but no doubt aware that it was all still in the balance, she did show admirable restraint.

Alex could feel even through her hair that she was trembling violently. Every inch he gained now was an inch gained for them both. She was quiet but panting heavily. He kept pulling her in, slowly, inch by inch until eventually she had come close enough to reach out and grab his shirt. With that, he let go of her hair and she twisted over so that she was facing down.

'Easy now, girl,' he told her as she scrambled up over his right shoulder. 'No quick moves. We're still in the game but we're in it together.'

As she climbed onto the bank, he pulled himself back even closer to the base of the sapling then swung his other arm, now free, over to grab the old tree root. In a second, he pulled himself up after her and with extra strain, the whole knot of roots and earth and sapling gave way.

Yet there were other plants now to hold onto and he scrambled up the bank. Below them, the tangle of tree, roots and dirt slid down the rocky channel and was quickly carried away over the edge.

From where they were, they could see the fall below and watched the sapling and roots shoot away into oblivion amongst the spray and rainbows.

Alex woke then in a fever of wonder, curiosity and residual anger. The intensity of these dream experiences was beyond anything he had ever known and it had all felt so astonishingly real. The last was a rerun from real life only a few months earlier when, under the most stressful of circumstances, he had first met Cara — but the rest before that had all been new.

How he did not know but the first dream sequence had enabled him to directly experience the story he had been reading. What it all meant he was not sure but he felt as if he was gaining insight into the early development of Thor's character.

Why he had relived the traumatic way that he had met Cara months ago in the wake of that dream of another world, he did not know.

Yet anger soon took over from wonder. The young Thor's inner battle came from a need to oppose sheer evil, and the sort of evil that could so cruelly sabotage the mind of a child left him in cold with rage. Yet there had also been the care and the beauty of the ethereal lady — and evil was not just in this other world. Was there not a poison in the veins of this world also?

Not just one child had suffered here but many — along with the very land which was the life of all —

children, men, women, wild creatures of the land and the ocean? Did the poison not creep silently through the world unhindered like an eclipse across the moon?

Was humanity not appallingly unmanned to so weakly permit its final enslavement, even after decades or lifetimes of exposure to a twisting, mind-numbing form of demoralization? He knew it but he also knew that he had not been fully facing it.

Only six chapters in and now Alex felt he understood the purpose of this tale, A New Star Ascends, however old or distant it was.

From the beginning, he had wondered how any novel or series of novels could be so important that it would be secured for thousands of years in a hidden place on a dead world but now he knew just how crucial its revelations could be — at least to any who gave a damn about peace and freedom.

Surprisingly, Alex found that he had slept through much of the night and the long flight from the US to Australia was nearly over. There was little else to do and the fifth title, Valhalla's Hammer, beckoned, pungent with the complex scent of danger and excitement.

A little into the third chapter, he realized that the pace had changed and that action had morphed into quieter dialogue, initially light-hearted banter followed by deep conversation. This made it very clear that these Aryan people were human in every sense of the word that counted. They joked around and laughed then did what they had to do, exchanging stories to help them work out the problems and find the solutions. They seemed to have a sense of the bigger picture and had far from given up on hope and duty. Yet they did not seem in any sense to be gods.

Thor, so cruelly poisoned as a child, had become aware as an adult that a deeper poison could insinuate itself on you by long association in the milieu of day-to-day conflict and that it too had to be kept at bay.

After a run of increasingly complex, violent and desperate missions, he had become conscious of the presence of a hidden trap — that violent action against evil was indeed both a poison and a drug, a mind drug that caused total immersion in its own way of doing things. It had a way of dominating ones thinking and tended to preclude the adoption of any other path more clever and inspired.

Vaguely on the lookout for a new strategy, he had been surprised to learn that one of his people had discovered something vital — something that might tie in with the visions he had been experiencing and the desire to explore a completely new way.

Alex read on quickly and was astonished to learn of the elemental spirits on Arya and the secrets of why they were so important to the Aryan people. Then there was Thor's first meeting with Odin. It was odd but tantalizing that they had not met before. At the end he sat pondering it all for more than an hour, until the hostesses came to serve breakfast.

Subtle mind powers were clearly something very important and real to Aryan people but it occurred to

Alex that even they were seriously limited by their preconceptions. Kane, the Shadow Circle technical wizard in these stories, knew the value of mental value-adding but was seriously limited by damage on an emotional level. Eirein was a hard sceptic, scarred by her own long exposure to violence, and Rolf, the mission coordinator, while open in theory to the concept of a mental transcendence, felt himself personally incapable, perhaps because of his own materialistic upbringing.

In a way, Thor was the man in the middle, the man who had often trod the middle path, and in the end, he was the one most capable of exploring the esoteric, arcane new path that was opening up to them all.

Still pondering these complex ways of balance and harmony and how they might have relevance for him, Alex was surprised when the jet entered a long slow banking manoeuvre and he saw through the porthole the familiar landmarks of the great emerald city below — the jewel green harbour, huge Botany Bay farther south, the tall sandstone cliffs, the golden beaches, the iconic Opera House, the wide span of the beautiful old Harbour Bridge and its relatively small stone counterpart over at Northbridge.

Chapter 3 — On Mountain Roads

The sleek old Jag turned over for a moment then purred. Getting on for eighty years old and still a kitten. Alex guided the long, low nose of the red E-type convertible out of the carpark and onto the road, wondering for the third or fourth time whether he should call Cara.

She was much younger than him; twenty-six to his fifty-two and a gut-wrenchingly gorgeous blonde — but when he had left for the US she protested more than once about how long three months apart would seem. Every so often, he found himself feeling guilty for being with her and wondered if her feelings were not solely founded in gratitude for saving her life — but this time he something changed within him and he rejected the guilt. She knew very well what she wanted and in any case, harbouring the guilt was a habit that spoke of placing emphasis on the destination rather than on the journey.

He wanted to call her now and it seemed the right thing to do but he also knew that he had to make up his own mind about these Time-Vault files, without her potentially pushing him one way or the other. Until he was clearer about it, she would have to wait — and it would do her no harm.

One clear principle had guided him even as far back as his early forties. If circumstances were complicated, keep things simple. Erring on the side of caution *could* turn into an obsession in middle age but in this case, the circumstances justified it.

The morning was warming quickly so he stopped and took the trouble to fold back the top. The sun and the breeze on his face would be welcome at least for the first half hour until he cleared the city.

While waiting in the terminal, he had scanned through the first few chapters of the fourth book, Wrath of the Thunder God, and discovered that Aryan Thor had developed a capacity for remote viewing, enabling him to home in on his arch enemy. Yet some unforeseen circumstances had complicated the hit, leaving the target badly injured rather than eliminated.

Not ideal, Alex thought. The remote viewing might be patchy at first but one could hardly blame the phenomenon for Thor missing the shot.

In fact, the big thing was that he had become clearer about the significance of the spiritual and more inclined to explore it — more in the sphere of focusing on the journey rather than the destination, if it came to that.

The book also discussed how having suffered as a child courtesy of the inimical Meccanat had driven young Thor to think laterally in ways both material and spiritual. Somehow, despite not knowing what caused it, he had learned how to use the pain in a positive way and it had compelled him to seek new sorts of answers in unexpected places.

The story evoked danger both to loved ones and to the wider public and the further Alex read, the more he became concerned that in having these manuscripts, he might actually be on thinner ice than he had imagined. Yet he passionately wanted to keep it, come back to it, work through the language a bit and maybe one day publish it — but if he did that, the cat could hardly fail to get out of the bag.

The files seemed authentic and he judged they were significant, even if they did read like fiction. They were observant and even very relevant in revealing how things worked even in this world. It was no wonder that the discovery had not been released and if he did put it out there, it could result in some very severe consequences. Even now, he felt trouble looming, though he knew not in what direction it lay.

Alex knew himself well enough to understand that whatever unease he was feeling would probably result in him calling Cara. Truth to tell, he had a lot of time for her. Blonde haired and willowy with lively light green eyes, you would have placed her as a cheerleader or something else sporty but in fact, she was inclined to make good use of her brain instead. Moreover, she appreciated that he used his. Damn, what was he doing driving away from her, now?

He pulled over into a garage not far from the freeway entrance and made the call.

'Alex,' she said, answering it. 'You're back?'

'Yes and no. I'm not stopping in Sydney. You alright?'

'Yeah, I'm okay. Why would you ask?'

'A lot of strange things have been happening lately. Just wanted to check.'

She paused a moment.

'Thanks. What's been happening? I've been thinking about you too.'

'You shouldn't be thinking about an old man like me.'

Cara laughed.

'You're twisted, Alex. Old man?'

'Well, I'm going to get old ... before you.'

'Didn't think you were the worrying type.'

'Okay ... you got me.'

'Sounds like you weren't going to call me then changed your mind.'

'Got me there too. How do you do that?'

'If you have to ask ...' she said with a little laugh, 'but what's up? You didn't actually say.'

'I'm not sure I should. Just got back from the states and I found something very interesting there ... something I've got to deal with now.'

Cara paused again before answering.

'Mmmm. New millionaire returns from OS with secrets. Thought you said you were too old but there you are, turning me on with mysteries and secrets.'

Alex laughed with her now.

'You seem to be the one with secrets ... fetishes you haven't told me anything about yet.'

'Don't turn it back on me. Cough it up. Spill the beans or I might have to get nasty.'

'All I can tell you for now is that it's reading material ... particularly strange reading material.'

'Reading! It must really be earth-shattering or you'd hardly even be mentioning it. Are you really going to make me wait?'

'Come down in a day or two?'

'The Snowies?'

'Yes, the Cove. You remember how to get there?'

'Of course ... though it has been a while.'

'Good place to read secrets. Spirit of the CIA in the winds.'

'Oh yeah, the disappearing CIA house? Like that is it?'

'Yes but more so ... much more.'

Cara shrieked in delight.

'Oh, no, can I come tomorrow? Tonight?'

'Tomorrow, the next day, suit yourself.'

'Actually, I can't come tomorrow ... leastways not until the afternoon.'

'Then you'll arrive after dark. There'll be roos.'

'Damn roos spoiling my private racetrack ... but didn't you say they don't have enough time to react when you're going really fast?'

'That's only with the ones sitting still by the road. If you hit one in full flight at speed it wouldn't be pretty ... and they're so damn unpredictable. A neighbour had their brand-new car stomped on a while back. Saw the roo and stopped but it jumped onto the bonnet, onto the roof and then onto the boot.'

'Maybe I can switch my appointment to first thing in the morning.'

'What?'

'Academic interphase.'

'That what they call it nowadays?'

'Professors always have to have a finger in the pie.'

'Not in this one.'

'Okay, they can starve.'

'Sounds good to me.'

They talked over a few practical matters for a little longer then Alex excused himself, having a long way still to go.

The drive was mostly boring freeway, even if it was in a nineteen-sixties Jag soft-top, but not long after Cara hung up and he got to the Monaro Highway in Canberra, that changed. Traffic banked up and before long, he saw that there were police guiding cars off to the side. They seemed to be looking for something.

When it was his turn, a team of police went through his car while another spoke to him. He wondered if they were looking for the USB drive but he had that on a string around his neck.

'Where are you travelling to sir?'

'I've been in Sydney and I'm going home.'

'Where to?"

'Eucumbene.'

'Nice. Do you fish?'

'A little. I moved down there more for the skiing.'

'You're lucky ... get all the good snow, I reckon.'

'What's all this about, constable?'

'Big crowd in Fyshwick, sir. They call it a protest but it looks like there's a good many infected amongst them. It's turned violent and we don't want any outsiders coming in to join the fray.'

'I don't suppose you do. They're bad enough to deal with on their own but if there's infected amongst them, the whole crowd could turn.'

'Exactly. You seem to be clear on both fronts, sir. Not infected, simply going home. You'll find the highway flanked with army and police for the next ten kilometres or so ... so take it slowly.'

'I was thinking of turning onto the Bobeyan Road.'

'That would be wise. Enjoy the drive.'

As the constable stated, the highway was lined with police and army vehicles, mainly army and he proceeded slowly. On the south side of Fyshwick, he could see over to the west and noted the large crowd. It was in fact huge and that could spell trouble.

Australia had dealt well with the recent pandemic wave — better than most, and this sort of thing was unusual. No one liked the methods used against the populace in these instances but most thought it was either that or an even more deadly chaos. The ones who really objected joined the protests.

Alex sympathized with them — but the recent manifestations of new covid were hugely infectious and the symptoms bewildering. Vaccines were completely ineffective. The symptoms were not lethal or even painful but sufferers' behaviour changed permanently in unpredictable ways.

Once past the melee, he did turn off onto the Bobeyan Road. It was curvier and more scenic and the weather was amazing — classic early-September invigorating; cool windy and bright with snow just visible on the distant main range.

Near Adaminaby, a left onto the Snowy Mountains Highway led to a right onto Middlingbank Road and then the last and best part began — the racetrack as he called it. He swooped down twenty-five klicks or so into the valley where it intersected Rocky Plains Road then climbed up again to the plains.

By then it was getting close to five and he had to keep an eye out for roos but even so, there were some long straights clear of trees where he could wind the old girl out. A serious rebuild and some clever mods had given it the wherewithal to tackle the climbs with ease and he had the will so where any clear view ahead allowed it, the plains reverberated pleasantly to the deep rumble and crackle of the big vee-twelve.

After a right turn near the old Rocky Plains school, he slowed down for the tighter curves and the farms, where old timers still occasionally moved cattle or sheep between paddocks along the road. Slower again, he entered Eucumbene Cove Road and the glistening lake became visible through the trees.

This was one of the largest lakes in the country but the Cove was only a small part — maybe a tenth of the total area, set apart from the rest by tall snow-gum-covered hills and a narrow water channel.

The sealed road capped the dam wall and on the other side, a varied assortment of around fifty houses, most of them elegant or endearing in some way, graced the hillside. Most overlooked the sparkling yet oftentimes moody and treacherous lake.

Chapter 4 — The World of Arya

Alex swept the E-type up the steep, winding drive and got out. He let himself into the house and went straight to the lounge. The fireplace was set and the log rack was full.

Two or three food items went from the freezer into the oven then he stretched out on the lounge as the flames began to paint themselves on the walls of the otherwise unlit room.

Just then, he remembered to call Cara and let her know about the protest. It could still be going tomorrow and she should know about it.

They had a brief conversation but she was busy with her travel arrangements.

After eating, he stoked the fire some more, stretched out on the lounge again with a doona and read with his computer on his lap.

On reflection, Thor's journey to his family estate in the wake of his attack on Helvig seemed remarkably like the quiet cruise he had just undertaken from Sydney to the Snowies, but Thor had spent it with Laseja, really Freja, who he had rescued twice in two days, while Alex had been alone on his journey.

Rescuing a damsel in distress had been done many times in fairy-tale and adventure scenarios or otherwise and for Alex, it had to be done really well to work. And it did, even if had been written a long time ago. For someone who had actually trod in those steps, albeit in different circumstances, it rang true.

A little later, he read that Desea was the principal city of Asgard. There it was. There could be no doubt about the Norse connection.

Asgard was one of two states on the largest and most populous of five inhabited isles on Arya and in the stories, it was clearly in a state of chaos, gripped by dark, predatory forces and torn by rebellion.

The predation was, of course, largely on women.

Attractive women in all great societies throughout time had been regarded as objects of value in specific, limited terms. That had not really changed. Few modern human societies had the maturity to properly understand the underlying principles that governed relationships and consequently, women were still hunted as prizes for men of strength, courage and initiative — as they had apparently been at that time of this story.

After pondering this element of hunting for a while, he was left wondering if the basics of human attributes could ever be changed. The main driving forces behind human interaction were after all founded in thousands of years of behavioural evolution and to expect people to abandon all that in the course of a couple of generations seemed like the quintessence of hubris.

Yet, for all that, the hunting of young women for exploitation was not exactly an ideal dynamic, even if there were those who were prepared to rescue them. A more positive dynamic *was* needed but that was most likely to happen more effectively if people did not expect change too rapidly.

Interestingly, Thor's choices had led to exemplary conduct both by him and the lady he had saved. A man saved a woman from danger and disgrace and did not pursue the immediate advantage he gained from having done so? So, what did she do thereafter? Blithely get herself into another compromising situation? No, it was different. In this instance, Freja went to the effort to find out as much as she could about the man who had helped her then went on to think carefully about how she could go about helping him.

Moreover, her feminine attributes and pastimes, being somewhat different to her masculine counterpart's, had equipped her admirably to help him in ways he could never have foreseen. Beautiful!

Art reflected admirable reality, Alex thought — not some twisted fantasy of unattainable and purposeless equality.

So, the elements of philosophy expressed in this chapter were a good foundation for a more refined, creative approach to life without a ridiculous degree of change. The seeds of understanding had clearly been there in Thor before he met Laseja, whose real name was Freja, but his life's work battling the forces of evil had repressed those seeds until a worthy feminine archetype appeared on the scene to work her magic.

The idea that exercising free will was more difficult and uncertain than many imagined had been growing in the back of his mind but she had drawn the full truth out of him by her willingness to listen, despite initial distaste for what she thought was a strange, radical concept.

In the end, both of them had an awareness of the conscious mind and were able to help each other draw higher consciousness out more in the ultimate expression of will and purpose.

Thor made it very clear in the following passage.

"'Our destiny could be many things wonderful and amazing but predestiny, as defined by the material conditions and situations of our lives, is but the basic structure, like a trellis for a vine, that makes destiny possible. It gives us hope, ambition and a sense of purpose. It leads us to the glorious heights we can only achieve if we give this life our all, rather than simply going through the motions.'."

It was a strange paradox to a conscious mind yet somehow it did ring true.

And then, shortly afterwards, Thor clarified the role of the divine in making this happen:

"After all, can we as limited mortal beings, have anything like the complete knowledge of the universe that would allow us to even set the most interesting, rewarding best possible goals?"

Then:

"With trust in the divine that events and insights will lead us to a worthy goal actually set by the divine, we are yet, in accordance with the twelfth key tang of Mindcraft, capable of making positive, constructive decisions along the way."

So, in life, as Alex had often thought, it was not what you did that counted but how you did it or, as he had thought before, about living the journey rather than waiting for the destination. This was especially the case for any mortal with a limited ability to determine what the best gaol might actually be.

Again, it had to be noted that at this point, Thor definitely thought of himself and referred to himself as a mortal. This 'Mindcraft' precept that he had referred to was one of a number of key elements of understanding in what was clearly a venerable philosophy and the idea of working effectively within a "limited freedom of will" framework left Alex in awe.

Events and visions would lead people forward and trust in the divine could create the right conditions for good progress despite their not actually knowing where they were going. It might also reinforce peoples' trust in their own ability to act in any given circumstance to fulfil their own destiny. God, the One, as they called him, gave humans brains to use but it was up to them to choose to use them and to work out how to.

Alex could not help but think that all the strange events of the past few days were drawing him forward mysteriously yet irrevocably into a phase of his life that would be critical for his own destiny. He, like Thor, had experienced visions or at least dreams that seemed to be telling him all this was important — very important. And he clearly also had a role to play. He would have to use his own judgement in dealing with this but unfortunately, everything currently seemed vague and unfocussed. He scarcely knew what to think.

Was this scenario all real, anyway? Were these stories of any real value in the scheme of things? Where would it take him if he let it run on? Most of all, was the world of Arya real or was it simply some popular tale left behind on Mars by an ancient astronaut because he liked it — or even because he was playing a practical joke on whomever might find it?

Ever since finding the manuscript, Alex's dreams had been filled with visions of strange places and things that he imagined were Arya.

Now, at home in his own retreat, his own castle of a kind, he slept and dreamt again of that much larger castle on a hill surrounded by tall snow-capped mountains. The entrance lobby could have held his whole house and he moved though it again in a daze admiring beautiful timber panelling, paintings — both portraits and landscapes, statues and every so often stands of spectacular bright metal armour.

Passing through the wide doorway at the other end of the corridor beyond a broad staircase, he entered another corridor at the end of which were waiting rooms, storerooms, a kitchen and other utilitarian facilities. With a thought, he willed himself back to the staircase and wafted up as if on a breeze.

On one side of the corridor upstairs was a vast and beautiful dining room with a table as long as a bus. On the other side was a comfortable loungeroom with a vast stone fireplace and he could feel the warmth of the flames across the room.

Deep plush lounges surrounded the fireplace and the high walls were adorned with velvet hangings and huge tapestries on varying themes. There were battle scenes, picnic scenes, party scenes and detailed portrayals of musical performances.

The floor was of polished timber but many plush rugs were strewn about all over the place. If these people were Aryan gods, they sure knew how to make themselves comfortable and enjoy.

Each time Alex woke to the sound of the wind or the creaking of his multi-level pole house, he returned to the castle when he fell asleep again. It was the most intense, lucid, coherent dream he had ever experienced.

Was it just a dream, he wondered, or was it in fact a full-on vision?

Outside the castle, several wheeled vehicles sat on the pink and white gravel drive. They were strangely but beautifully designed, evocative and expressive of their main purpose but fundamentally not unlike modern cars of Alex's experience. Then outside, Alex began to look at the sky, and it had a different quality — a deeper more indigo blue and in it he could see two moons, in different phases — one new and the other near full.

It was Arya!

With that realization, he dreamed again but this time he had one of those strange falling sensations again, as it had been when he had dreamed of this place while on the plane back from the US.

This time, with strangely counterpoint relevance, he was falling through the open air and behind him, the jet that he had come from suddenly exploded into thousands of pieces in a great ball of smoke and flame.

Looking back in front of himself, he saw that he was wearing some sort of flight suit and strangely, he seemed to know where he was headed.

In a strange melding of memories that were both his and Thor's, he was aware that events had moved rapidly and panned out with unfortunate consequences for those of his enemies still in the air plane — the turbo-wing as Thor called it. He had ignited a small explosive charge up near the cockpit to cover his exit but somehow the resulting fire had gotten into the fuel lines.

Thoughts about Shadow Circle mission protocols came into his head but Alex knew these were totally Thor's. Surrounded by enemies aboard the turbo-wing and facing the worst, he had had no choice — and the modest thermal blast had thrown everything into confusion, making it possible for him to push past the others back towards the rear hatch.

Clear of the blazing wreckage and gliding steeply away from the deadly chaos he had unleashed, he had begun to turn over the harrowing details of the operation gone awry, both from a strategic and a human perspective. He had been successful yet regretted the unforeseen loss of life.

In the wake of that, Alex felt that he should begin to concentrate on the present but then everything changed. In an instant, he appeared in a dark cavern aboard a small boat floating on some underground lake. All around were the screams and flapping wings of evil bat-like creatures. One swooped in close and in moments he began to feel very strange.

It was all very confusing. A female voice called out to him in fear but the voice was inside his head. There were two girls in the boat with him but both were looking at him strangely is if he was not making any sense and they were not calling out.

Then he was somewhere else again, running across a busy road then down a road towards — towards the girl who had called out in fear! He could see the girl running away into a dark little side alley from unknown assailants.

Waking then under the first light of the sun, Alex jumped up and felt horribly cold so he threw some fresh kindling onto the smouldering coals, wondering why his awareness in the dream had jumped so many times — from the air to a boat in an underground cavern with the bat-like creatures to a strange road in a city trying to find a girl who had called out in fear.

Damn, but the Aryan world with its deep blue sky and its two different coloured moons seemed so real. Never before had he experienced a dream so convincing, so all out in detail ... so real.

After a quick breakfast, he took his mountain bike up the steep track behind the chalet and quickly got warm. Patches of snow still lay about from the last fall even lower down but it was not long before he was scrunching his way up the hill through foot deep snow, glad of the willing power of the electric assist.

At the top of the first rise a view of the lake opened out to the right and the morning sun shot off it in many directions. A few patches of mist were lifting still but the warmth was growing quickly.

Up at the top of Bald Mountain, you could see all over the lake and across to the main range mountains to the north, west and south. It was thrilling being up in the snow country with the wind beginning to rise and snow plumes lifting from the tops of the distant main range.

At last Alex began to feel that he was truly home again, grounded and ready for whatever might come.

When he returned and opened the door at around eleven, the phone was ringing.

It was Cara, of course, and she sounded happy.

'Alex, I'm on my way,' she told him.

'Good, I'll get some work done before you get here. Don't push that beast too hard. I want you here safe.'

'Killjoy. I'm fast and safe.'

Alex got a fire going in the main lounge where he kept his two grand pianos — one his grandfather's 1849 Bechstein and the other his almost new Bechstein, both of them gems in different ways. He sat on the lounge and read further, hoping to knock over most of the rest of the book in the five or so hours he had before Cara got there. He would read it more slowly again later but for now he wanted an overview. He and Cara would talk it over and he needed to be able to direct the conversation — the analysis.

Clearly, Thor was a person of significance in this society. Unknown elements had sabotaged his very mind probably because he had been born into a key noble family. As an adult, he had returned to the family castle with some reluctance no doubt because of his painful early experience of it. Yet it was beautiful and the narrator described it as exactly like the one he, Alex, had seen in the dream. How could he have known what the castle in the story would look like?

Escape to a high place from invading troops followed — then another vision of mind transference, remote viewing or astral projection; whatever you wanted to call it.

A great secret was revealed then — a hidden place where astonishing elements of the old, now banned, religion were revealed — secrets that lit Thor's spirit. With them, he could fulfil his destiny — free his world at last from the secret noxious power holding sway over everything and everyone.

This revelation affected Alex more deeply than he thought possible. He had been driven almost to despair in recent times by the growing hysteria that gripped this world as well as the ever-increasing tendency towards the worst moronic conformism.

It was why he lived for the most part in a remote place and more than ever, he was glad not to have to work for a living. The moral sickness was everywhere and he was tired of it — tired of the stupidity and the professional incompetence these attitudes seemed to generate, tired of the lies and emotional manipulation and of the endless creeping bullshit.

Yet he also knew that he had taken the easy way out compared to Thor in his world with daily vengeance and black ops. Had he made the wrong choice?

The next few chapters of Valhalla's Hammer stirred the flames further because Thor and his people took the rebellion to more extreme levels with an initial mission to break out political prisoners and free the imprisoned Queen Fjorgynne of Vanaheim (the smaller state to the south of Asgard).

After a while, the anger made him tired and he drifted off into a deep dreamless sleep, strangely blank for first time in many days.

Chapter 5 — Cara's Adventure

On the way through Canberra, Cara found that the protest Alex told her about had grown even larger. Even from some distance away, it seemed that government forces might be having difficulty containing the crowd.

Cars and trucks seemed to be racing around to and from the area dramatically so she proceeded slowly. Lots of people were walking beside the road and quite a few were hanging around in groups. A few kilometres before Fyshwick, the traffic slowed even more and was soon almost at a standstill. After a few minutes it was at a complete halt and a wave of people came up from the west of the highway.

Cara suddenly felt alarmed. The crowd was moving quickly and yelling loudly. A little farther down, they were attacking cars and there were no signs of police or soldiers. She would not just wait there to get attacked. There was no going back now because the crowd had also filled the road behind her and she had no illusions about them respecting how they might feel about her and her flashy ride. That was one of the big problems with wealth. It placed you on the side of authority whether you approved of it or not.

Now a part of the crowd was moving fast towards her and she decided there and then to sidestep the line of traffic ahead. She pulled off onto the road verge and stiffened her resolve.

Accelerating hard, she tore up the side of the road, swerving out of the way of several cars trying to do the same ahead of her and tooting the crowd repeatedly to get out of the way. By now she was moving fast enough that no one would want to risk being hit and they let her through. She wondered about that response for a moment then realized that it might also be the sheer aggression that she had displayed. They might think she was one of them — a crazy.

Her heart pounded like it was coming out of her chest as she swerved here and there between the verge and the turf, the Aston's throaty vee-eight bellowing belligerently as she did so — but eventually the crowd thinned and she saw the Bobeyan turnoff. A wave of relief flooded through her.

The crowds were behind her now and there were signs of a good day ahead.

***

Alex woke again and began reading the final pages of the chapter in which Thor blew the huge Vanaheim military facility to high hell. Just then there was a toot outside. He went to the back door and saw Cara's Aston Martin coupe in the driveway.

She got out and by the time he had his shoes on, she was there, holding him.

'I literally blinked an eye and you were in my arms,' he told her.

'I thought I was the witch,' she replied with a sweet mischievous look in her eye.

'That'd be clever. Wish for someone then make it seem to them like they did the wishing.'

'Couldn't it be mutual, you know, like telepathy?'

She noted that his eyes looked more green than blue today and was reassured by that. A relationship was nothing without feelings.

'I'll buy that. Good trip?'

'Roos all behaved themselves. Can't say the same for the drivers ... on that Jindabyne Road.'

'Par for the course. You should have come the back way.'

'You like the back way?'

'Don't be wicked.'

'Why not? I missed you.'

'Bring any food?'

She slapped him on the butt.

'I did. You can get it out. I've gotta go.'

Alex smiled and went to the Aston. The boot was full of groceries god bless her. He had not asked her but she must have guessed that he would be focused on other things. While he was putting things away she came downstairs in a white towel bathrobe and poured herself a gin and tonic. Her hair was wet.

'I had a quick shower. That's a long drive.'

'Feeling better?'

'Yes, except it feels a bit cold in here. Do you have a fire going? It's really cold out there.'

'It is a chalet.'

'Chalet with no snow.'

'Not now. Maybe tonight. There's a change coming through. Had a fire going but I let it burn out.'

'Hope you've got plenty of wood to keep me warm.'

Alex grinned and put the last of the cold things in the freezer. She came and stood over him.

'Did you just say what I thought you said?' he asked her, holding her around the middle and pulling her in tight.

'What if I did?'

'Well, I can see we won't be working too hard on this project, at least not tonight.'

'I saved myself for you.'

'Why would you do that?'

'I ... I like you.'

'Like me, like you want me around?'

'Well, not all the time of course. That's the worst thing about all the young pips my age. They either don't want to be there at all after they've taken you, or they want to be with you every minute of the day. There's no in between ... no happy medium.'

'Boring ... but I'm not making any promises.'

'Good. Don't. Good formula for misery.'

Alex clicked. Pro. Mise. She was going through a word discovery phase. Good on her.

'You really in the mood?'

'Probably not. Just getting comfortable.'

'Thought so.'

'You're very understanding.'

'No, I'm getting comfortable too.'

'Lounge looks good over near the fire there.'

'Alright, I'll get it going again.'

Alex went to get kindling and set the fire. It was going in minutes and he added some bigger logs. With that done, he sat down and Cara joined him, settling herself on top of him with a warm smile.

'Lucky you're a lightweight.'

She slapped him and slipped off to the side then pulled his head down to meet hers. They kissed, lightly at first then more exploratively, making the most of every sensation. After a few minutes, she relaxed, cradling her head on his shoulder and he could see that there were tears in her eyes.

'What is it?'

'All this time I've been worried.'

'I'm fine. This is strange, this story, but there's no danger ... as far as I know.'

Cara looked at him and smiled, her green eyes bright.

'That's what I like about you. You don't let your ego lead you around. I meant that I was worried you'd come back and I'd find that you never wanted it to be any more than ... friendship ... or that you'd found someone else.'

'And that's what I like about you.'

'What?'

'You don't mind telling me how it is. You wear your heart on your sleeve and don't care if anyone sees it. Most young women are so guarded now. Think they've learned all the tricks and all they're doing is doing themselves out of love.'

'I wondered when you'd notice.'

'Noticed a while ago but couldn't seem to believe it. I mean, I've been through the mill, sweet thing. Always hoped there'd be one out there and didn't know what to say when I found one.'

'One?'

'Human without bull.'

'Well, we make a good pair then, don't we?'

'No bull.'

Cara sat up a little, not entirely convinced.

'So, what's this mysterious project?'

'It's a flash drive I found on Daytona Beach a couple of mornings ago.'

'What's on it?'

'Thirteen manuscripts ... stories about another world.'

'They're good?'

'Yes, they're totally different but there's more. There are other documents with them. One in a strange language and a script I haven't been able to find anywhere on the net. Then there's the report and the analysis.'

'What report?'

'They came from Mars ... the stories ... from a vault in a lava tube.'

Cara laughed.

'Now you're pulling my leg.'

'No, actually ... I'm not.'

'But I haven't heard of anything like that.'

'Neither have I ... and the thing is, I found them in this secure case on a beach that had been broken open in a storm ... smashed on rocks by the look of it. It looked tough and expensive and this report, it's very detailed and professional.'

'What does it say? What's the conclusion?'

'The report writer thinks it's on the level.'

'Well of course it's on the level. Came from Mars, didn't it?'

Alex noted that she wasn't laughing, even in her eyes.

'True.'

'No, I meant do they think it's a real story ... like a history or fictional style account of real events?'

'That's what it says ... but if it's all an elaborate fraud then that's what it would say, isn't it? But I've been having all these strange dreams.'

Cara sat up and leaned forward putting her head in her hands as if putting her thinking cap on or at least putting blood flow back into her head.

'Dreams, huh? Any official letterheads?'

'No, but if it did fall into the wrong hands and they were trying to keep it a secret, the absence of a letterhead would at least cast doubt on it if someone brought it into the public eye.'

'Yeah, but that wouldn't be the end of it, would it?'

'What do you mean?'

'If someone brought it into the public eye, they'd pursue them, wouldn't they? I mean this would be NASA wouldn't it? A US government agency. If push came to shove ... I mean, you don't even know how it came to be in the ocean, do you?'

'No.'

'It wouldn't have happened by chance. Either someone stole it or ... I don't even want to say.'

Alex frowned.

'I didn't think of that ... but I didn't do anything wrong.'

She looked at him quizzically. She seemed to be asking him whether he meant legally or strategically and for a moment he wondered if it was telepathy.

'Could I have a look at the drive?' she asked.

Alex got up and took it out of the lap top bag.

'Here,' he said, handing it to her.

'Thanks. It does look unusual and quite a bit larger than other things like it.'

She took the cap off. There was a dim red flashing led that showed in the semi darkness.

'Did you know about that?'

'Didn't see it when last I had the cap off. The light in the cabin was bright.'

'Maybe you should dispose of this or hide it somewhere.'

'Maybe, but not tonight. If they haven't homed in on it yet then they aren't looking ... at least not in Australia.'

'It might take a couple of days for them to confirm that it's no longer in the US.'

Alex stood stock still.

'You might have a point. I've got some old lead flashing in the storeroom. I'll wrap it up in that until tomorrow morning. Then we can get rid of it.'

'Where?'

Alex went to the window and pulled the curtain a bit.

'See that big hill over there? Bald Mountain, it's called.'

She came and stood beside him.

'I see the silhouette. Why so far away?'

'Well, it's not very far really, and that way we can see if there's any unusual activity going on there.'

'Tomorrow?'

'Early.'

'Maybe you should try to talk to them.'

'Not sure about that. Take a look at it first, at least. It's a game changer. They were hiding it for sure. The report is dated relatively recently but I've actually been following Perseverance's progress. It was temporarily out of action almost six months back for a few weeks which could have been when they found the lava tube and investigated it. And if they lost the manuscript and didn't want to admit to it, they wouldn't put out the word that it's lost ... which they haven't.'

'They do like to hide important things, don't they?' said Cara.

'And where would we be if we just handed back a potentially history making document when we do know that they hide everything they can.'

Cara huffed.

'Why do they do that, anyway? People say they don't want to promote panic in the population ... but really, who would panic?'

'You're right. It's not about that. It's about control, like everything from mortgages to fake news to all this ongoing hysteria over disease and so on.'

She leaned back and sighed.

'Okay, I'll take a look at it but you should be careful what you wish for. If it's more interesting than you then you're out of luck tonight.'

'Ungrateful minx,' he said, pulling her back close and loosening her dressing gown in the process. 'I let you in on the secret of the century and you're brushing me off now after teasing me into a frenzy.'

She fell back into his arms and let the gown slip. They kissed and then she got up, the gown untied.

'This had better be good.'

Chapter 6 — Joint Venture

Later, Cara snuck a look at the laptop on the dresser and the file that was open on it. She discovered that Alex had been reading a chapter where Thor went in single handed and destroyed the main military base of Almaris in the region of Vanaheim — male-oriented high stakes adventure but then she scrolled back to the beginning. At least she would be able to share one part in common with him when they got up in the morning.

It read like something out of a war or spy novel and she found it hard not to think of these events happening somewhere here on Earth. In truth it seemed perhaps a little too 'boys own' to be a true account of real events but flipping back and flipping forwards she soon found passages that were more introspective and frankly, more productive. Thor, it seemed, was not the simple stereotype action hero.

His connection with the elemental spirit of ether was both restorative and reassuring in the face of so much death and destruction and his conversations with the newly revealed elemental spirit revealed deep and subtle elements in his character.

A long day it had been for Cara and not long after she began reading the next chapter, which revealed a little of the hidden enemy, she succumbed to sleep and began to dream. Like Alex, she began to dream of Arya and somehow knew that it was Arya, not Earth.

Still a little nervy from the drive and the prospect of seeing Alex after a three-month separation, she was half awake, half asleep and the dream was as lucid as any she had ever experienced.

Strangely, first up she saw one of the hidden enemy — an individual of a strange race — vampire-like with long white incisors, pale skin and cold faces. She walked through Vanaheim Palace, a grand edifice of beautiful design and finish, and encountered the grim enemy in greater numbers. They seemed to approach her with intent then passed right through her oblivious.

In the end, she relaxed and explored the palace from top to bottom, looking out through various windows and doors occasionally to see mountains on one side and the distant sea on the other. Eventually she found hidden rooms in which people were being tortured and she tried desperately to free or rouse them. None had any reaction to her presence and in the end, she could only feel a deep sorrowful desperation.

Awaking in the early hours of the morning, she clung to Alex like there was no tomorrow.

'Nice to be wanted,' he observed just after dawn. 'Lucky it's cool here though.'

'Don't be a beast,' Cara replied in a way that made him truly sorry for what he had said.

'You alright?'

'Dreams. It's strange but I think they were of Arya ... like the ones you had. There were vampires or vampire like beings ... and they were cruel.'

'To you?'

'Nooo! They didn't seem able to see me, thank god ... but I could see what they were doing to others ... in this castle ... and that was so beautiful ... strange gothic like architecture but with a twist.'

Alex shook his head in amazement.

'Oh my god! You were there. It's just like that ... towers going up in a rising spiral. I couldn't have put it better. Were you reading after I went to sleep?'

'Yes.'

'That'll teach you. Treat it like a job I think and we'll just read all this during the day.'

She smiled at him.

'Well, it's not really day yet properly, is it?'

'No, it's not. I can guess ...'

'I believe you can.'

'Excellent cure for vampires.'

'Yes. Poor things, all they desire is blood.'

Later, not long before midday, in fact, Alex jumped up and took a shower, ending it with the usual cold blast. When he came to the kitchen, he spun around the TV, switched it on and found that he was just in time catch the midday news.

A few mundane local items took up the first ten minutes but then, just as he was mixing his passionfruit, elderflower and pomegranate rejouvier, a piece from the US caught his attention.

'The body of a senior NASA researcher, missing after being abducted on her way home in Florida, has been found washed up on a beach,' said the news anchor. 'Police say she was abducted by an unknown assailant, who is also missing. Sarah Hilton's SUV was found abandoned near a breakwater and it is presumed that both she and her abductor were washed out to sea by a freak wave during last week's destructive storm. It's unknown what the motive was for the abduction but reporters at the scene have noted that a large-scale search is being conducted in the area even after Ms Hilton's body was found. NASA has been tight-lipped about her role but according to reliable sources, she had a security tail that followed her to and from work each day.'

Alex sat down on a nearby stool and let out a low whistle from between his teeth.

'What is it?' Cara asked, coming in just at that moment and starting to make coffee.

'They showed footage of the breakwater ... and the beach near Lighthouse Point.'

'What?'

'The beach where I found the briefcase. The woman ... she was a NASA researcher ... swept off the breakwater during a storm ... her and her abductor.'

'Oh no!'

'Drowned, poor thing ... probably with the abductor but they made no mention of the briefcase ... only that the search was ongoing ... even though her body had been found.'

Cara frowned.

'Well, of course, they're looking for the crim as well.'

'Of course ... but they said it was a very large-scale search. Larger I think than would be for the body of some crim.'

'But wouldn't they want to know whether he was really dead or not?'

'Sure, especially if they thought he might have the briefcase.'

'So, you really think she was the owner of the briefcase that you found?'

'Same beach. Same day. Damn right I'm sure. NASA, my love. It had to be. God but these stories must be really important. They must be the real deal.'

Cara's eyes widened.

'Actually found on Mars?'

'Yes.'

'In what form?'

'Inscribed on thin gold plates, I believe.'

'How did they get them back to Earth?'

Alex smiled.

'They mightn't have even bothered. I imagine the robot scanned them all and sent everything back to Earth digitally.'

'Oh of course. They were on a USB drive, weren't they?'

'Yes. A good one but this one clearly of Earthly manufacture.'

The kettle was near boiling and Cara took it off the base. She poured a cup and added the rosehip and hibiscus mix before sitting on the lounge next to the kitchen area.

'Then there seems to be only one really crucial question,' she said, after taking a sip.

'Mm?'

'Whether this was just some sample of culture left by an alien race ...'

'Or whether it was an actually history.'

'Let's read some more.'

Alex switched off the TV and came over to her.

'Yes, why not? Everyone wants this ... and we're the ones who've actually got it.'

He went to get the computer and they sat next to the window on the lounge in the sun.

After he had perused the next couple of pages a little, he turned to her and said:

'It doesn't seem fictional to me. I mean I know it's written like a story but this is Thor, after all ... Thor and Freja and Odin and even Fjorgynne ... and to be honest, these stories aren't anything like the traditional Norse gods myths. I mean, just for one thing, there's all sorts of things and names and places and people that were never mentioned in the myths.'

'And they're not gods ... at least not yet ... fighting a rebellion against inimical forces ... and using guns instead of swords ... or a hammer.'

'Kind of fitting, wouldn't you say? But actually, Odin has already given him the hammer.'

'Oh really? Yes, maybe ... but if they did end up as gods or godlike beings, they had to struggle to get there. It actually seems a lot more real than the myths.'

Alex sat up.

'You've got a laptop as well, haven't you? Why don't you read the earlier books and I'll keep going on this one?'

'Sure.'

'You'll catch me up pretty soon. I'm nowhere near finished all of this and there are still a few that haven't even been translated yet.'

'I wonder what they are.'

'When I've done reading what I can, I'll use the translation code and do it myself.'

'That sounds like fun. Hopefully I'll have caught you up by then and we can work on it together.'

'Sounds like a plan.'

So, Alex gave her a copy and they read on through the afternoon, stopping only to get a fire going and to have a brief dinner together.

Cara was more and more impressed as time went by and occasionally looked up to meet Alex's eyes or make a comment about something that got to her. Reading on through the evening she went on to the second book and by eleven had finished it.

'I can't believe what I'm reading,' she said in the end.

'It's too much, isn't it?'

'Too much!'

'I think we should get out for a walk before turning in ... clear the head. Moon's out.'

'Cold out, though, isn't it?'

'Then it'll clear our heads.'

In fact, it did do that but it also got the blood going and by the time they got back from a turn around the block, Cara had moved closer and Alex was making the most of it. When they got back, he led her to the bathroom and they took a shower together, making love in the heat of the water flow with only a dim orange bulb lighting the steamy air.

Chapter 7 — Ancient and Beautiful

The following day was overcast and it soon began to snow, not unusual at all for that area in early spring. It did, however, come down in unusually thick and heavy flurries with quite a blast of wind behind it. Soon there were drifts near half a metre deep.

Alex kept the fire going from a big wood-pile behind the house and they read on given that they could scarcely have watched anything anyway with the satellite dish completely covered. The house was warm but Cara was happier snuggled up reading in bed.

Since she had some catching up to do, Alex decided to take notes and create new files for the books to which he made changes as he saw fit. The writing was good but his impulse was to alter things for the better wherever he could.

He had not decided what to do yet but ever more as time went by he developed the sneaking suspicion that he would publish these stories as his own work and damn the consequences. The US government would have hidden it forever and for no good reason. People had a right to know just as they had a right to live as they wished.

Cara was onto the fourth book 'A New Star Ascends' and he was onto the seventh, 'Quest for Dragons', coming to terms with the idea that there could be elemental spirits and intermediary spirits that could take the form of dragons or people as or when it suited them. It damped his spirits a little for he could no longer see how these stories could actually be real events, however long ago or far away.

He asked Cara what she thought and she was not so dismissive.

'Why not?' she said.

'Really? Dragons? I mean dragons maybe ... but ones that can change form into humans?'

'Again, why not?' she replied. 'They're not supposed to be material beings, are they? If they're a spiritual entity, who are we to say what they could do?'

'I don't know. It just seems a little far fetched.'

'What, the existence of spiritual beings? How could you possibly say for sure that there are none?'

Alex looked at her curiously.

'Because none have ever said hello to me.'

'Again, how would you know?'

'But why would they hide what they were?'

Cara started to look exasperated.

'The spiritual code, of course, silly. You can't ever hope to become a spiritual being without having real faith that it's possible.'

'Oh, I get it, if these beings flaunted themselves, we could never become like them because we could never develop the capacity for faith.'

She smiled.

'Now not so silly.'

'And there aren't bad spiritual beings?'

'I don't think so. It wouldn't make any sense. There might be bad spirits in the sense of being lost souls but they have no control over their form or their fate.'

'So, Sauron wasn't a spiritual being?'

'Oh, don't talk to me about Tolkien. Love him and hate him. He opened up vast vistas of imagination but logic wasn't his strongest suit.'

'What about the bad guys in these books?'

'Not spiritual. They live a long time didn't you say ... but die in the end.'

'But not Thor and his people, surprisingly. Only a hundred and fifty, max.'

'Yes, that's strange, for gods.'

'Well, these people don't seem to be gods. It seems like Thor is a born leader but not a god. He gained powers in the end in part because of his relationship with the spirits but he's not really godlike ... not yet.'

Like him, Cara played the piano so in the afternoon they played duets on the old piano and the new, back to back.

In the evening they cooked an excellent pair of eye fillets serving them up with fresh corn, Brussel sprouts, butter and a tasty onion, tomato and tarragon hash.

***

Back in Sydney, a young woman, a second cousin of Cara's, was living a completely different sort of life. Taylor had allowed herself to get a little too drunk at the Pixie Inn on boisterous Oxford Street. Four vodkas in the first hour affected her manner and attracted attention — the wrong sort.

A heavy set, low slung type, Garron, had gone there to sell speed but he had some coke laced pot and had a good idea that it would be just the thing for the careless hottie.

A freckled strawberry blonde, she looked like just the type to welcome the right sort of offer — but he had other things on his mind. Sometimes, he let go and forgot the money, setting his mind instead on things that few would want to think or even hear about.

'Like a smoke, hon?' he asked casually.

'Whad've you got?'

'Weed, babe. It's good. Nice and sticky.'

'Show me!'

'Not here!'

'You're selling?'

'Gotta make a living ... but the smoke's on the house. If you want some goey after that ... fifty.'

'Sure.'

'Come with me,' he said, holding out a hand.

'Where?'

'Back door. I know the guard.'

When they made it to the back door, it wasn't even open. There was no guard and Taylor spun around on her heel. Too late, too slowly though, because he was ready and slapped the side of her head so hard that she lost consciousness for a little. He let her drop to the floor and unlocked the door. Returning, he picked her up and slung her over his shoulder, slamming the self-locking door behind him.

Outside it was dark. The alley was poorly lit and there was a yard opposite with grass and a few trees. He was not inclined to want to wait even a little so he took her into the yard and tore off her panties. She groaned and looked up. He had not even taken his pants off. There was a long knife in his hands and he had a strange, cruel look in his eyes.

Taylor screamed but he slapped her head hard again with his left and lunged towards her stomach with knife in hand. Just then he felt a blow on the side of his head and a shock of light filled his brain.

Taylor looked up, trembling, not knowing if this new dark figure would be even worse than the last.

'Who are you?' she cried.

He growled.

'Don't worry. I'm not here to hurt you ... but I should give you the almightiest spanking you've ever had.'

'Why?'

'You're drunk ... and stoned. Why would you come out here with someone like that? Get up and get the hell out of here. Did you drive here?'

'No.'

'Then I'll walk with you until you find a cab.'

'I want to go back inside.'

The dark figure shook his head.

'Have you got a death wish?'

She shivered.

'No.'

'Then let's find you a cab.'

'Okay ... but really, who are you?'

'Just ask the Wolf. He doesn't like young girls putting themselves in danger and sometimes we keep an eye on these sorts of places.'

'The Wolf?'

Every one knew of the Wolf Pack, she thought — but what were they doing here?

She followed, timid now, realizing just how stupid she had been.

***

In the morning it warmed up quickly and most of the snow was melted by eleven. Alex fired up the old gold eighty series Landcruiser he kept in the shed and they took a back track up into the mountains.

There was still snow up there, one to two feet deep nearly everywhere but the venerable beast had locker diffs and a lift kit. Alex had dropped the tire pressures before they set out so the snow was no big deal.

Up on the main range it was beautiful. The air was crystal clear and the sky as blue as Alex could remember. There was a fair cold breeze outside but warm inside the cruiser. The snow gums were mostly clear of snow because of the wind and their greens, greys and oranges added a warm hint of colour to the white blanket.

About half way up to the main range, Alex stopped near a peak and walked up to the top on the pretext of taking a leak. There was a small cairn of rocks at the top and he pulled a few stones off it.

In his pocket, he had a small plastic box and within it was the original USB drive that he had found on the beach in Florida. He placed it in the hollow and moved the rocks back into place on top of it.

'It's so beautiful up here,' said Cara, wide eyed, when he came back to the Landcruiser. 'I've never been up on the range like this, except to ski ... and it's different on the ski-fields.'

'Yeah, nothing like this.'

'Up here, I've almost forgotten about those stories.'

Alex grinned, accelerating the vehicle away up the track.

'I know what you mean. They're hard to ignore, aren't they?'

She glanced at him curiously.

'I've kind of been trying to.'

'Yes, I'm with you. Can't really figure out where it's all headed to, so I feel like holding back a bit.'

'Yes. Does that matter?'

Alex cocked his head.

'Maybe. Every so often someone gets the chance to make a difference in the world. Could anyone really refuse the opportunity if it smacked them in the face? I mean it doesn't happen all the time, does it?'

'Would it make much difference knowing this?'

'Don't know yet. I'll have to see what Thor says about the matter.'

'How's "Quest" going?' she asked after they had enjoyed a comfortable silence for a few minutes.

'I'm near the end. Nothing special yet. Just an out and out adventure story that one. And I've poked through the next two and they're much the same. Great fun to read but if you want to know what these people are really about, I'm thinking the next three after them will tell the story. I've translated the titles and the summaries and those later books are about when Thor rules the world ... after his successful rebellion. Look at a man when he's got power ... then you'll know him.'

'So, you've taken a sneak peak ahead with the final books?'

'Only a little ... but yes, I am looking forward to them. I imagine he'll get to the nitty-gritty in "Peace of the Hammer".'

'Why?'

'Oh, just the title. It's intriguing and suggests a fairly tough approach. Then the last one is "Bridge Over Time".'

'Yes, talk about intriguing. Can it be about the Rainbow Bridge?'

'I hadn't thought of that,' said Alex with a light in his eye. 'I'll have a bit of a look when we get back.'

'If it is, will that help you decide?'

He looked hard at her.

'You mean if it's about Earth and what to do? You bet. If it is about Earth, this is something that will need to be told. It would change everything. In truth, I don't know why I didn't look at that first.'

'Who would know where to start? You started at the beginning. That makes sense.'

'Yeah ... let's get back. I've done roaming around up here in the snow.'

Cara grinned, her generous green eyes lit with pleasure, for indeed she wanted to know all that she could now, just as he did.

It was slower going downhill than it had been coming up and more nerve-wracking as well. Some parts were steep with crazy fall-offs and the traction was far from perfect. Yet in the end, they got back in the late afternoon and stoked the fire.

After an early dinner, and reading for a while next to each other, they talked again.

'Have you really considered the consequences of releasing this?' Cara asked.

'Alright. Go ahead and publish and risk the ire of NASA or do nothing and miss a huge opportunity as well as keep a massive secret from the public. I mean it's just possible they'll find me because they can track the storage device, anyway.'

'Weren't you going to get rid of it?'

'I did.'

'When you went to pee?'

'Yes.'

'How could they link it to you even if they did find it?'

'Satellite images, maybe. Who knows? Anyway, somehow I just don't care anymore ... so why not stay a step or two ahead of them if we can?'

'It is important. If we know more about our true history, it will shake the grip that all sorts of bad things have on people. If that goes far enough, who knows what people will demand in the way of freedom?'

Alex nodded.

'What you said. It's even more important than I thought. We should definitely get it out there.'

'Is that an offer, Mr Jamieson?'

For a moment he was back to his old wary self but then something softened within.

'Well, yes it is ... if you can stand hanging around with a cantankerous old grouch like myself.'

'You have no end of funny ways to describe yourself, old man.'

'Is that a yes, then?'

'It most definitely is. That's the advantage of being in business ...especially with the family. I can take time off. They'll just think the obvious.'

'What?'

'Do I have to spell it out?'

She leaned in and kissed him.

'Oh ... but I can only offer you a cut of something that might go nowhere.'

'I have more than enough money already, as you know. That's not the issue. I guess I wouldn't mind sharing in the notoriety.'

'And the trouble?'

'I know a few people, myself ... not to mention dad. They won't be able to come after us in a hurry.'

'Maybe not. Don't be too sure.'

'If they do, we're in it together and we'll deal with it together.'

'Fact remains, though, I was the one who smuggled it out of America. I did use my twin brother's passport, though.'

'Why?'

'He disappeared a few months ago. Bad breakup and he just left everything like that behind, with me. Still, it won't do much to put them off my scent, considering he's such a close and obvious connection.'

'When it comes to publication, I could be the go-between with the publisher and we could use a female pen name. It might confuse them for a while.'

'I'll think about that ... but I really think I'd be better keeping you as a hidden asset ... maybe for when the going gets really tough.'

Chapter 8 — The Last Five

After four full days together, Cara had caught up with Alex and they read the ninth book, The Ice Warrior War together, each one reading aloud alternately until they finished.

Then, that evening, it came to translating the last five and Alex decided to look through his uncle's files again. He seemed to recall him talking about creating a super clever translation program given that languages were in large part like codes.

After half an hour looking through his exhaustive file catalogue, he found what he was looking for and copied it onto his computer. It installed in moments and he opened the first file. Within a minute, it was complete.

'Your uncle was clever,' Cara said generously. 'Most translation programs are online and the ones that aren't are pretty basic.'

'It looks pretty good. The intro is clear and the language nice.'

They translated the next three files straight away and for a while, they scanned through them, searching for things that might be critically important.'

In the twelfth book, "The Glory of Power", they came eventually to a chapter about the shared code of Mindcraft and its material benefits for leadership.

'Our grand poohbahs might benefit from this,' said Cara after reading Thor's speech to the leaders of Niflheim.

Alex laughed.

'Too right they could,' he agreed. 'Our leaders, here, and the leaders of all our major nations. No wonder so many things go wrong.'

'Yes, no wonder. The Aryans really sorted this. It all makes such good sense.'

'I wonder if it lasted.'

Cara wriggled a little.

'I guess we'll find out.'

'I particularly like these seven elements of constructive social interaction ... regard, curiosity, communication, trust, honour, vigilance and yes ... of course ... courage ... the courage of convictions ... moral courage.'

'It's interesting that it all starts with regard,' said Cara. 'It depends on finding that which we admire in someone else.'

'Yes, to establish a point of commonality. It's so obvious but no one in our society has codified the obvious and where it is not, once the obvious transitions to the subtle, the links are lost.'

Cara turned and looked admiringly at Alex.

'Yes, so they are.'

'And then, a little later, Thor explains his approach to the question of faith ... and he calls it High Magic. How unlike the basic warrior Thor we have known from our Norse myths!'

'A complex character.'

'Very.'

'It all seems to lean on focusing on higher ambitions and on true desires.'

'That, I can relate to. What else has meaning, in the end?'

Cara smiled alluringly.

'Loving, of course.'

'Oh ... totally, of course. When you think about where it all leads.'

'You don't have any children, do you?'

'No. Liz seemed to have something against it. She's a strange woman ... in many ways.'

'Strange not to want children?'

'Well, unusual in that regard and strange in others.'

'So, you have nothing against the idea.'

'Heavens no! But you just can't push a partner into something like that. How about you?'

Cara shrugged.

'In good time. You know, when you're ready, you're ready.'

'Love before marriage, marriage before children.'

'Who said anything about love?'

'Oh, god no ... dirty word that one.'

That was said with a grin and was received with a sharp slap on the arm.

'Dirty indeed! Sex is one of those naughty, nice dualities that Thor was talking about ... the kind that Idrasil uses for the achievement of higher goals.'

Alex grinned again.

'The positive view recognizes the limitations of the physical world but relieves us of any despair about it by offering the meaningful context of it being an essential catalyst for spiritual growth.'

'My god, I think that's word for word from what we were just reading in The Glory of Power. Do you have one of those ...?

'Eidetic memories?'

'Yes, one of those.'

'I do.'

'Well that does it. It would be a terrible waste for you not have any children.'

'And it's not the only good quality I have.'

'What else is there?'

'I have a very good nose for brandy.'

Cara kept a straight face.

'I know someone in France who could use that.'

That night, Cara and Alex went to bed early and they were asleep before midnight. The night was still and calm and dark and as silent as only the high country in Australia can be.

At some time early in the morning both began dreaming about Arya again but they soon realized that their dreaming included each other and with that blazing realization came a shared lucid dream of epic clarity and beauty. They were in the gardens of an estate beneath a beautiful castle that could only have been Castle Valyria. The trees were old and large and the shrubs brimming with flowers. No one seemed to be around and they had the place all to themselves.

After a while talking and laughing and kissing and admiring the garden, they decided to go inside and look around. Again, no one was there and they ranged from room to room ever upwards until they found the grand suite of the landlord, who was of course, Thor's brother Balder.

The chamber was amazing with rich beautiful wooden furniture, not too ornate but not plain either and the room had plush dark blue velvet curtains. The walls and ceilings were painted cream with gold trimmings and the floors were rich red timber.

A large window gave onto a balcony that overlooked the gardens and much of the rest of the estate but the bed beckoned and they lay down on it literally in a dream. Touches led to kisses and kisses led to more touches and soon they were naked together on the great bed of the Duke and Duchess of Deor.

Anyone who has ever loved someone in a dream will know that it is impossible to describe but over and above those incredible sensations, they had the crazy knowledge that they were both awake in another world and there together, wholly and consistently.

In truth, the experience was like none that either had ever enjoyed and it went on like that for what seemed like forever.

Yet in the end it seemed they slept and the scene changed again, dream within dream within dream.

It was late afternoon and they were high up on a mountain in the ice and snow with a couple of other people, one of whom looked like Thor's brother.

Both Alex and Cara were aware of each other and knew within moments that they were on some sort of a glacier.

'This is some strange place on Arya that I haven't seen before,' Alex told her.

Cara nodded and seemed to understand him but also seemed more intent on experiencing this high, beautiful place on another world.

The glacier was not very steep but it was slippery. Cara seemed to be a young girl aged about ten and in light spirits she stepped onto the snow, spinning around in childish delight, then found a patch of ice and dropped with a thump.

With firm snow beneath his own feet rather than ice, Alex felt secure but moments after Cara fell, a whole large section began to move beneath her — presumably on an ice layer beneath — and already well onto the glacier, they began to move also.

At first it was quiet but then they moved faster and the snow buckled and shot up in bursts where it slid over large lumps of ice or rocks. One by one they all fell down as it became impossible to maintain balance. The roar of the wind alone was huge as they gathered way but the ice and snow beneath them thundered with the deep voice of an angry mountain.

Thor's brother soon became separated and in the turmoil of wind, ice and swirling snow, Alex could not see the others. Several times, he saw Cara dip down and nearly disappear beneath the increasingly loose surface so he made an effort to roll over in her direction. After a few tries, he perfected the technique and came within range.

Cara's face and body sank again beneath the surface but he grabbed the back of her pack and held on. Spreadeagled and holding himself rigid, he did not sink and was able to pull her back up again. Thereafter, holding hands and keeping their bodies spread wide, they were able to float.

After the first minute they were travelling fast and a light mist of powdered snow rose about them. The deep roar around them drowned out any possibility of speech, but thoughts of wonder and delight were somehow there and reassuring them both, at which point they looked up and around to see snow and ice rippling around them in a mesmerizing rhythm.

The sky above was a deep indigo blue shot with the first evening stars. Snow mist shot up all over the place in spirals that every so often refracted light in such a way that they formed brief images like ghosts in the mist — faces, trees, ocean waves and serpents — before flicking away in a flowing trail into the gathering darkness.

A wild and wonderful ride it was and the initial great speed seemed to go on far longer than it should have but the grade of the glacier eased around half way down and they slowed. The wind settled and the flurries of swirling snow were left behind.

Their eyes met and in that moment, there was another abrupt change of scene.

They were in a large chamber and it seemed to be deep under the ground with a high vaulted stone ceiling but Alex could not see Cara. He was with another, a large powerful man with a kindly, generous face.

Around them were strange, vampire-like people and Alec knew at once that they were Ice Warriors. They were dancing in a circle with a strange and beautiful pulsing rhythm and they chanted along with it in a deeply hypnotic way.

Each ring nearer the centre counter rotated with the one before, creating a hypnotic effect in the visual parts of the mind that lent greater majesty and beauty to the scene. Wafts of various kinds of incense, sweet, pungent, fruity and spicy, drifted through the air.

For what seemed like minutes, they watched and listened, compelled by their senses, until Thor's companion shook him slightly and Alex woke as if from another dream.

In the morning, both Alex and Cara woke together and looked straight into each others' eyes.

'Was that real?' Cara asked, getting up.

'So, you really were there too?' Alex replied.

'What a castle. What beautiful gardens. What a beautiful bed! And what a story after that!'

'How can it have happened?' Alex asked. 'I mean, I've never heard of anyone doing that ... sharing a conscious dream ... let alone doing it in a world twenty thousand light years away.'

'And probably in another time. Everything we've read about in those books must have been a very long time ago if it happened at all.'

'It seems impossible ... yet we both experienced the same thing.'

Cara moved closer to him again.

'What does it mean for us?'

'Well, if we can keep doing things like that ...'

'What if we can't?'

'I think I'd like to keep trying ... if you don't mind.'

'No, as it happens I don't mind. I mean who wouldn't?'

'You'd have to be crazy.'

'Maybe we are.'

'Nice kind of crazy that.'

'Yes.'

After a shared shower, they made love again and in its intensity, it seemed completely different from the day before. There was also a depth, a spirituality about it that was deeply compelling.

Two days later they had finished reading the thirteenth and final book of the Reign of the Dragon set and they were staggered again by all the questions answered in it.

Thor and his people had travelled to Earth or Midgard as they called it, and established a society of Aryan races on it — humanity's forefathers! Some of them had gone through various stages of development and had become godlike in their powers, enjoying apparently eternal life, virtually unlimited space travel and even the instant materialisation of physical objects that they desired or needed.

Not all could be given immortality and deep rifts had formed in Aryan society over the question. In effect, the gods had been forced out of Arya over that matter and had lived for thousands of years on Midgard, until later again they were forced to leave.

Many of their children and children's children remained there, however, and there had been a whole history that went from around twenty thousand years in the past to about eight thousand years in the past with its own history and mythology. That, apparently, was the subject of the other series of six books, The Rings of Fate, which although mentioned was not in the files.

Soon, they translated and ventured into a smaller text called 'A Guide to Arya' and learned more detail about the language and culture of these people.

Around this time, Alex created a new version of the books with different names and all the references to the Norse gods deleted. He thought it might be best to publish it that way but it was still up in the air.

During the time that they spent absorbing all the elements in the guide to Arya, Alex and Cara were so deeply affected by being intimately attuned to each other that they made a rapid decision to get married.

'This world was in chaos back then and individuals suffered just as they do now,' Alex had observed to her, 'but now our world suffers more and we have just been lucky as individuals not to suffer too much.'

'Are you thinking what I'm thinking?' Cara asked.

'I'm thinking that I am. I'm thinking that this could change at any time and that we should make the most of the time we have, while we're healthy, free and independent.'

'We won't be independent any more if we're married.'

'That's different. We're independent of the things we want to be independent of. And we cooperate constructively with each other so you can't call that co-dependent. I believe that's a bit of a rarity.'

'The right things brought us together and we've worked together in the right way.'

'We have,' Alex replied.

'What more could we ask for?'

'Love, money, two homes, a project to work on together ... and even the thrill of imminent trouble. Yes, what more?'

'I'm not just going to elope with you, though. Don't get the wrong idea ... I'm not hung up on the wedding flimflam but I do think that at the very least it's a social thing ... family and friends and all that.'

'Perhaps you're right. I won't argue with it anyway.'

'Good. Then when?'

Chapter 9 — Tradition and Ceremony

The when was only a couple of weeks later because without excessive amounts of the said flimflam it could all be organized to Cara's satisfaction fairly quickly. No news good or bad came about the books but Alex had the feeling there was some unusual activity at times around the hilltop where he had hidden the original data storage device. For that reason, he was happy enough to spend a little time in Sydney anyway.

Cara's father, Grant Laughton, had a girlfriend, Genie, who owned her own waterfront house not far from his in Double Bay.

Genie took special delight in arranging everything but stood back graciously whenever Grant's children had anything they wished to contribute. Brad, Cara's brother, and Felicity did want to contribute a lot, carried away as they were by the warm ties of matrimony shared with another couple in the family, even if that couple differed a little in age.

Given the numerous other ties she had through the family construction business, Cara also knew a host of people. The same was true for Alex as a journalist, and many of those were keen to find out what he had been doing for the last couple of years.

In the end, the afternoon wedding in the grounds of the Laughton mansion was an occasion that rang nearly all the right notes. There were some present amongst the many guests who seemed to be more curious about their circumstances than seemed right for the occasion but for the most part the company was excellent.

A wide lawn spread down from the mansion to the jetty and boathouse with pleasant shrubberies and a pool and waterfall in between. There were flowers everywhere and tables overflowing with food and drink. The music was live with a full grand electrified piano and mixed classic and rock instrument accompaniment.

Day turned to night under a clear sky in the increasing warmth of spring and the only thing Cara thought was missing were the brilliant stars you could see in the evening high up in the mountains.

One of Alex's old flames, Karen, was there and would not let go of him. Cara began to be worried but her father caught her eye and shook his head.

Alex was, of course, only being polite and he excused himself not long before his parting speech.

'Normally, the bridegroom carries the bride over the threshold to the blissful future that awaits them,' he began when he spoke to the expectant crowd late in the evening, 'but in this case, as we older men do, we just smack them on the backside and get them at a full run up the stairs. No, I'm not yet up to pace with the teaming hormones of my young bride and I do get worn out ... but I don't think too many of you will be feeling much pity for me. I salute my lovely bride.'

Cara rolled her eyes a little but took the whole bragging brutalist thing in the spirit of humour that it had been intended, as did nearly all of the well-primed and now grinning guests.

***

About a month later, close friends of Cara's from France who had not been able to make it to the wedding arrived and were keen to spend a week or two with them in the Snowies.

In a good year, the upland spring wildflowers were a sight to behold and this year promised to be one of those. Blake and Justine Ormond were accustomed to seeing and experiencing the best, old wealth as they were, and the spring wild flowers of the Snowy Mountains were a favourite of theirs.

Alex's little chalet was not exactly luxury nor large in terms of a typical billionaire's taste but it did have character and a spectacular view over the lake.

Blake had no objection to roughing it for a while, knowing well that there was always a cost to living in the lap of luxury every moment of life. Justine shared this perspective, for indeed it had won her over when she first met him.

So it was that they chose to inhabit the tiny loft above the upstairs lounge room and therein enjoyed the best view of the lake that the house offered.

Most of the reading and editing of the books had been done, converting the Norse gods in the series to just another race of humans living on another world far away, but when they first read it over in that form, Cara and Alex felt that something vital was lost. The old version with the Norse gods had been kept and they decided to return to it.

Around this time, they used their friends, in readings during their evenings together, as beta testers for the books in their final iteration.

'Where did you come up with the idea for the Norse Gods being mortal but finding the means to become immortal?' Blake asked Alex one evening after a long walk up on and near spectacular Mount Jagungal, the most substantial solitary peak on the alpine range.

Alex had never really enjoyed lying but in this case, he knew he had to be inventive. It would not do to have too many involved in the secret and it might not do them any favours knowing it either. All the same, it rankled.

'You know, I didn't really start off with them as the Norse Gods,' he responded eventually. 'I was looking to portray a culture under threat in a similar way to our own yet with the key difference that it was a pagan culture rather than a Christian one.'

'You were trying to tease out what might be the weak points in our culture by hypothesising one that would react differently to a similar set of challenges?' said Blake with ready perceptiveness.

In truth, Blake had had many conversations with Alex and Cara on a wide range of subjects over several days already so he did already have a good idea where the focus lay.

'Yes, it seemed like the obvious alternative ... so build a world around a different set of values and see how it responds to the same sorts of challenges. Then, when the whole thing seemed right, the whole Norse god thing just popped into my head.'

'So, you converted the stories to people with the names and experiences of the Norse Gods. That must have been difficult.'

'Not really. I knew quite a bit about them already and Cara had some excellent insights.'

'It must be exciting being an author and creating these worlds from your own inner being. I know it's a big thrill for me and Justine to be involved like this, just hearing it all now, before anyone else.'

Alex gulped and wondered how many times he would feel guilty to lie to people and hear such reactions in the months and years that lay ahead. More and more, he felt like his life was becoming a pack of lies without any true meaning.

'Yes, my life's dream,' he said, but Blake was surprised by how dour he sounded.

Blake enjoyed sailing, so on the following day, Alex took him out on Eucumbene on his beast of a catamaran — a near twenty-foot NACRA. It was only a light breeze of about seven or eight knots but that was perfect for the big rig on the 5.8 with its thirty-foot mast.

In truth, Blake began to suspect something was up when they were sailing, because Alex seemed to change so completely out on the boat. It was like sailing was his heart and soul thing and it was the only thing that could fully relieve him from a growing inner darkness.

Whistling along with one hull up well out of the water and both men right out on trapeze was always the sort of thing that would put you right in the moment but

Blake had been sailing with a lot of guys and this was the deepest, most complete transition he had seen.

'You love your sailing, huh?' he said later, when they got back into the shore.

Alex looked sharply at him.

'Shows, does it?'

'Yep. That and something else.'

'What?'

'Not sure yet.'

'You sure you wanna know?'

'We all run the same sorts of risks, fella. We just think we're different.'

'Maybe.'

Alex frowned for a moment.

'Alright. I think I can judge that statement to be made on a higher level. I think you might even have an inkling what you're in for.'

'That bad, huh?'

Alex met his eyes.

'The books aren't mine.'

'Not Cara's either?'

'No ... and they're not just sci-fi fantasy novels. As far as we can tell, they're actually histories.'

Blake slammed a hand down on the ute bonnet.

'Histories? Thor and Odin? How could that be? How would you know?'

'Remember some gal in NASA was abducted and she and her abductor ended up in the drink during a storm in Florida?'

'Yeah, I heard about that. It was strange.'

'You think that was strange. I was there the next day on that beach and I found a briefcase.'

'Her research?'

'She was a translator. I found the USB drive in the case, which had been smashed open on the rocks.'

Blake shook his head in wonder.

'Just the USB drive? It would have been encrypted.'

'Sure. Looked like the bigger case was made to contain it. Tailored padding. I was there in Florida to wind up my dead uncle's affairs and he was a cryptologist.'

'Talk about being in the right place at the right time ... and with the right skill set. Even so, you're not really happy about it, are you?'

'No, you picked upon that alright. Yet, somehow, overall, it all seems to fit. I know that it's important. I just don't like being such a passive player.'

Blake nodded.

'I get that but sometimes life offers you up things you don't think are quite fair. It's a hard mistress and doesn't seem to share the niceties of principle we like to hold onto.'

'Good way of putting it,' Alex replied, 'but then there's the practical dilemma of dealing with NASA over time.'

'Wouldn't there have been some sort of tracer on the drive?'

'Probably ... but it isn't here anymore ... not the original.'

'It could be just coincidental. It might not have been the NASA woman's bag or drive.'

'Then why was it encrypted? And all the other bumph in it talked about how the scripts were found in a lava tube on Mars. No, it's the real thing.'

'And you're just going to release it eventually as your work?'

'Mine and Cara's ... from her dreams.'

'You're mad. They'll come after you.'

'Don't see how they can. Cara's old man's pretty high up in the scheme of things around here ... and they've no right to keep it secret. It's life changing. You think about it. No more Catholic Church monster, no more religious delusions, no more sense of isolation for little old planet Earth. No more thinking that we live, we die and that's it. It changes everything.'

'Then why aren't you happy?'

'I don't know ... maybe I'm just uneasy about the upshot.'

Blake and Justine decided to stay a couple of weeks longer but it became hot around mid November — and Eucumbene was best when the weather was cold. The two couples decided to rent a place down at Bermagui overlooking the beach. They were in it together now.

Alex trusted Blake more than any other man he had known in a long time. He trusted Justine too. She was a good sort. Now that they knew, they wanted to know what they could do to ensure their friends' safety but also wanted to ensure the best outcome for the project.

'When are you going to release the first book?'
Justine asked.

She and Cara were lying on the sand while their
men were out body-surfing the breakers, a couple of days
after they arrived and had settled in.

'Next month. A couple of weeks before Christmas.
It's getting close. All of them at once, though.'

'Does the publisher know?'

Cara laughed.

'Of course not! This is something we can only ride
out ourselves. If they knew they'd freak out and cave the
moment they felt any heat. But they're quite a small
operation and they'll make a killing.'

'You'll cop all the trouble then.'

'Yes.'

'If it comes to legal bills or anything like that ...'

'We're covered ... and we have the best lawyer.'

'Still, anything we can do ... just let me know.'

'It's just good having you in on the secret. I felt like
I was going to explode and then Alex told Blake ... just
like that. I couldn't believe it ... but I was glad.'

After lunch, the two couples took a drive then a
walk on a remote beach. It was peaceful and beautiful but
the surf had become even rougher and there were no
lifeguards so they decided to take a walk up the next hill
and along the coast a little.

There was a small track that led up through dense foliage over the first low hill then down into a valley and on up another larger peak on the other side.

'Do you think this is just an animal track?' Justine asked as they began to climb the steeper rise.

'No, it seems a little too worn and the branches look like they've been pruned back,' Alex replied. 'There always seems to be some sort of track even in these remote coastal areas.'

As they crested the next hill, they could see smoke rising from a higher hill a little to the west, above and away from the sea but not out of sight of it.

'What could that be?' asked Cara. 'I hope it's not a bushfire starting up.'

'No, the smoke is sort of thin and curling ... looks like it's coming from a chimney.'

Soon, they came to a junction and took the turn up towards the smoke. After only a few minutes, they came to a clearing and saw a small stone and wood cottage hidden in a cleft in the land. On the front balcony stood a dark-haired and very intense looking woman, who greeted them with a smile.

'Welcome,' she said. 'It's a nice afternoon for a walk ... but it's rather a long way in here. Would you like something to drink?'

'Thank you,' Cara replied, 'but we have water.'

'Oh, I can do better than that. Come on up and I'll fetch you some glasses.'

Chapter 10 — Witch of Alden

Up on the balcony, which was really more of a deck, wide and comfortable, the four found that there was seating for them all and they suddenly seemed able to let go and relax there without a care in the world.

The lady excused herself and got up to go inside after she had introduced herself to them all. Seria was her name. Justine soon followed her in, finding the cottage beautifully finished with timber panelling and a number of stone features, including a large stone fire place. It was a little dark but in a pleasant, warm sort of way.

'Can I help with anything?'

'No, I make pretty much everything myself but it's all quite well organized. You'll like this, it's a sort of ginger beer ... with a little kick.'

'Oh, just a little I hope. I love your cottage ... so out of the way and so pretty. And it looks like it's much larger than I thought.'

'Yes, there's quite a bit hidden by the trees ... and even some underground.'

'You're ready for anything then.'

'I'm ready for life. I have been for a long time.'

Justine thought then that she looked ageless — not innocent and untouched but without any overt signs of aging. In her early thirties tall, willowy and sleek, she always did her best to look after what she had to keep physical deterioration at bay. It took a lot of work.

Seria was either like that or there was something magical about her because few who looked as young could have quite her intensity.

'Do you live here alone?'

'Yes, but I have many friends.'

'I'll bet you do.'

'Thank you!'

Seria poured some drinks into large glasses on a tray.

'Bring the jug if you don't mind.'

'More ginger beer?'

'Oh, it really only does have a little kick.'

Outside, the others greeted the drink bearers warmly given how hot it had become. They had walked a good distance, as well.

'What made you settle here?' Alex asked Seria after all the glasses were passed around.

'I inherited the cottage. It's been in the family for generations.'

'It does look quite old ... and beautiful.'

'It will never be built out ... I hope.'

'Let's drink to that.'

Quite suddenly the sun was shining in a way none of them had experienced before and the air smelt sweet like the breath of heaven. Flowers on vines around them seemed to open and the distant sound of the waves was like a gentle hush for the soul.

Seria poured Blake and Justine another drink and they were already too affected to notice that she had only topped up theirs. She smiled reassuringly at Alex and Cara and somehow, they knew she had no evil intent. After several minutes of remarkable quiet, Blake and Justine got up and walked inside.

Blake held Justine's hand, not so much reassuringly but with the sort of deep pleasure that neither had not felt in a long time. They walked into the house and explored, somehow knowing that they were welcome, and with each step some new delight came before them. Light like auroras played around them and they had strange visions of beautiful places far away. There was some sort of music in the background but neither could identify it. Walking quietly from room to room for some time in a sort of trance, they were completely spell-bound by all that they saw, sure that there was a deeper meaning behind it all.

After a while, listening to the sounds of nature in the golden sunshine, Alex met Seria's eyes and saw that they were an astonishing purple colour. With her dark brown, silky hair and ivory skin, she had quite a remarkable appearance.

'Your ginger beer is very pleasant,' he said in a way that was not so much accusing as interrogatory.

'Yes ... and I did give your friends an extra glass. They will enjoy it but I must speak with you and they cannot hear what I have to say.'

Alex and Cara exchanged meaningful glances.

'You are on a path,' she continued, 'that will change many lives ... not just your own. You, Alex, are more aware of this even now than you would care to admit.'

'What could you know about our paths?' Cara asked.

'The world ... no, this existence, is much more complex than you imagine. There are forces at work that you do not currently understand and events to come that will shake your world to its foundations.'

'Our world ... this world? You are not of it then?'

'No, I am not, I am ... we are ... natives of the world Alden ... a pleasant, pretty world like this but very far away from here.'

'We?'

'You see before you two people in one. Our races grew close in symbiosis from very early on and we have greater strengths together, in all sorts of ways, than we would have alone.'

Alex was both shocked and alarmed and sat bolt upright quite suddenly.

'Somehow I believe you,' he said. 'You're like that race in the Stargate series. The ...'

'The Goa'uld ... although we are more like the Tok'ra. Yes, our presence was seen as a vital part of the plan to prepare the human race for important revelations that would come.'

'Then why are we here?'

Seria smiled knowingly.

'For many reasons, not all of which I can apprise you of at this point. There is so much to take on, so much to understand. The main thing for you to understand is that there are numerous powers in this galaxy vying for control and not all of them are benevolent. You are here to learn more and I am here ... we are here to ultimately expose and eliminate these destructive forces.'

'From our world?' said Alex.

'Yes, from your world and from others ... but there is more currently going on in this world of yours than you might think.'

Alex frowned.

'If you and your race are here in force,' he said, 'why have you not destroyed the evil that has clearly dominated in this world for so long?'

'It's not simple ... and like you, we are not overly powerful. Neither are we many. We have had to wait and watch and slowly guide limited numbers of your people into countering the powers at work in this world. Like you, Alex. You know that you're selling yourself short. You've known that for a long time but you're still uncertain about taking that final step.'

He glared at her. How could she know this about him when he scarcely did, himself?

'I don't know what you mean. What more can I do?'

'You know what the enemy is yet you stand on the fence.'

'The evil god that the Cathars spoke of?'

'They were not far from the truth.'

'Why are you telling us all this?' Cara asked.

Seria turned to face her directly.

'As I said, you have already involved yourself. You know about the ancient past of this world and of the distant gods of Arya.'

'Yet you said you were not Aryan. You are from Alden?'

'Yes, a world that is not even close to Arya, yet is far closer to Arya than to Earth. We are not a powerful or aggressive race yet we have learned to travel in space quite effectively. We keep ourselves to ourselves and do what we can when the more powerful races, like the Aryans, fail to perceive what they should.'

'You do what you can to help people?'

'Yes, and to undermine those who would dominate them.'

'Yet you seem to have failed in that, here.'

'Not as much as you might think. We are small in numbers here but we have made plans and those plans have born fruit. When the crunch comes, the enemy will find much more pitted against them than they thought possible.'

'And you're going to tell us about these plans?'

Seria got up and moved over to the balcony rail, overlooking the ocean.

'Not all. Some ... for you must not dive in any further, unprepared. You will have read all about Arya and Muspellheim and Niflheim by now. You probably know more about these places than I do. What little knowledge we have came directly from the leaders of Muspellheim, whom we came to know after the Aryans were banned from Earth. It is incomplete ... and like many people, we wish to know just what was in those NASA files. It might help us.'

'What if you are not what you say?'

'Not benevolent?'

'Yes.'

'I think you know already.'

'Yet you did drug us.'

'Not really. Your friends more so, for good reasons, but what I gave you simply clears the neural pathways of interference. The more you have of it, the less resistance to the true energies around you. Blake and Justine are simply seeing the world as it truly is ... but in truth this is how they cannot see it when they need to survive in it. There are no harmful side effects and the experience will fade only gradually. And in any case, they have sufficient wealth to sustain them without a rapid return to the demands of the world.'

'Very well. So, go on. Tell us what you know.'

'We followed a ship into the rift. We believed it to belong to a grasping, violent race called the Aereons and we wished to keep our eyes on them. We were not sure if the rift destroyed both the Aryan vessel and the Aereon one so we waited until a ship returned. Then we waited for another Aryan ship to go and followed them. Of course, we had lost touch with the Aereon vessel and gave up the chase, returning as soon as we could so we could report back to our people.'

'It sounds as if you, yourself were there,' said Cara.

'Indeed, I am old ... but not that old.'

'How old?'

'A little over a thousand of your Earth years.'

That took a while for Alex and Cara to absorb and when they looked up again, Seria seemed to be waiting for them to get back on track.

'You must know so much.'

'Much ... but there is more that I need to know.'

Alex nodded.

'So, your people returned.'

'Yes, we kept an eye on Earth and when we began to see how badly things were going wrong here, we came and established a presence. We tried to find and destroy the Aereons but they are wary creatures and we decided we would have to wait. The Aryans did not seem to be interested and we did what we could. That was around three thousand years ago.'

'Then you were born here?'

'Yes. We have always wished to maintain a low profile. It seems the better way ... for us. So, we did not wish many comings and goings of spaceships to be seen and reported on. We built our presence here quietly and once we were convinced an evil regime had established itself here, we began to put our plans into action.'

'What plans?'

'All in good time, Alex. This is just the beginning ... but in essence, the organization of your people against the threat. We have one true stronghold of power, here, and I will tell you more of it later.'

'Then are we coming to that time?' said Alex.

'To the time when the Aereons might be found and destroyed? Yes, many things are coming together and I think we are near that time. A time when many things will be set to rights. A time as of the elves and dwarves of old in Master Tolkien's mythology. For when we first came to Earth or to Midgard as the Aryan gods liked to call it, there were races that fit this description and used those names. Then in a break of only a year or so, they completely disappeared.'

'I have wondered about those other stories,' Alex told her. 'They're referred to in the Reign of the Dragon books and they're called The Rings of Fate. They follow the Reign of the Dragon ... but we don't have them. I wondered if they would speak of real events.'

'Yes, they do, from what I understand ... even perhaps concerning the rings of the elementals ... but for the time being, you must keep this secret and perhaps, if you would, help me when I ask you to. Don't worry, I would not ask you to do anything very difficult. I can even tell you what it will be. When the time comes, I'll simply ask you to go and see some people in Sydney in another important organization that I did not start but have been fostering. You will tell them that they need to listen closely on their short-wave radio to make contact with Zephyr ... with our people in Scotland. I will send one of my people to you soon ... and he will be our go-between. He will tell you when to go to the others and will introduce you.'

Alex felt like he was about to step off a precipice but in truth, there was no going back.

'One of yours ...'

'An Earth native. One of our organization.'

'You mentioned the rings of the elementals. Why?'

'Because they may still exist in this world. Again, keep that possibility very, very secret ... at least from people who have no need to know.'

'What of the Reign of the Dragon books? Should we withhold them? We had planned to publish them soon.'

Seria came and sat down with them again and leaned in close to Alex.

'I would ask only that you let me read them first. Let me come to your place and read them before you go to the city and release them.'

Alex turned to Cara.

'If Seria's right ... let her,' said Cara. 'If she's just a crazy woman with delusions, what harm could it do?'

'She doesn't seem crazy to me.'

'Nor to me. So, let her come with us today and she can read them. How quickly can your read, Seria? There are thirteen novels of about two hundred pages each and a guide book of about sixty pages.'

'I believe I could get through three a day easily enough. If you can have me for four or five days ... then let's do it.'

'Very well,' said Alex with a sigh. 'It's done.'

'Before we go, I have a gift for you.'

Her hand went into a pocket at her side and she withdrew two metal discs embossed with ancient looking runes. They appeared to be made of silver and were fixed to silver chains.

'These have subtle properties, my friends. They will help you remain unseen and hidden to electronic devices designed to detect people ... and they will aid your nerves in difficult circumstances. Please accept this gift as you face a difficult journey.'

'Don't see the harm in it,' said Alex, mystified but willing to accept that there were things beyond his understanding.

Cara nodded and took one, and Seria handed the other to Alex.

Blake and Justine stayed another week, along with Seria — a little over four weeks in all and in the end, Blake's corporate minders were becoming frantic — calling every hour over something or other.

By the time they left, they had read all of the books in the series and were as astonished by the content as Alex and Cara had been. Seria was not astonished but there were many items of information that were useful and revealing to her.

'I hope you will keep me in the loop,' Blake said to Alex, the evening before they left. 'Seria clearly thinks there are big things in this and I don't disagree. We've got to do a few miles in the next couple of months but I check my email three times a day.'

'Better you than me.'

'Don't worry, I keep a tight rein on it.'

'I don't think anything much will happen until a little after the release, though.'

Seria also returned to her home the next day. Cara took her back while Alex went over the books in a sort of loose scanning process one last time.

Chapter 11 — The Good and the Bad

The book release was on December 10, a Wednesday, which Cara thought fitting given that it was also her birthday — something her editor, Carmen Richards, had insisted on exploiting when she discovered that it was so close in any case.

The launch was held at the Domain near the central Sydney foreshore, in the open. Cara's father had paid for the best caterers and the food was good. It was also plentiful and the launch was open to the public so it drew lunchtime crowds straight away.

Carmen knew well that she was on a winner but how much of a winner she had no idea. From the first moment there seemed to be a sort of hysteria associated with the books and, on release day, her well-written and heavily practised speech took on a strange quality of unreality, which could not have suited circumstances better if she had planned it.

'I don't know when a series of thirteen books has ever been released on one day before, fourteen if you count the "Guide to Arya",' she said to the crowd by way of opening. 'Guide to Arya, you might ask? Where is Arya? Well, to tell you the truth, I don't know. It's out there somewhere. It has to be. The Reign of the Dragon books are so real, so pertinent, so timely that they could scarcely be fiction.'

Alex looked at Cara intently.

'What have you told her?' he asked, sotto voce.

'Only that they came from my dreams,' she whispered back. 'I think she's drawn this conclusion all by herself ... but what harm can it do? Why hold anything back now?'

'Promotion is the name of the game.'

Cara nodded and retuned into Carmen, who by the looks on the faces of the audience, had apparently just said something a little "out there".

'I've known the authoress for many years and she is mostly definitely not crazy ... so friends, when something extraordinary like this comes from her subconscious ... with all the incredible detail and history ... and it all tallies broadly with what we know about the past, including mythology ... what could anyone conclude but that it has come by mystical means into her mind?

'What can we conclude but that this place and these people exist or existed somewhere currently unknown ... although we are given an approximate location some twenty thousand light years from here on the outer rim of the same spiral arm that our world occupies.

'What can we conclude but that Thor and Odin and Freya and Vrig existed and came to us here on our world via a wormhole that they called the Rainbow Bridge. What they say about this in these books and what they do, both on this world and on their own, I will leave for you to discover for yourselves. I can say no more, other than that this life changing.

'We have here fifty copies of each of the series and a couple of hundred of the very first ... The Thunder God Arises, all signed by our dear friend, Cara Laughton, or should I say now Cara Jamieson, who has used her married name as her pen name in acknowledgment of Alex's key role in drawing out these dreams, hammering out the fine detail and editing all these works with the passion and professionalism for which he has been so well known.

'What a couple we have here ... what a stellar literary couple. I give you ... Cara Jamieson and Alexander Jamieson.'

Cara was no wallflower and thrived in the limelight. That invitation was just like a big box of fine chocolates after several quality liqueurs. She stepped forward with a huge smile and beckoned Alex forth to share it.

There was a long spell of applause and it felt enthusiastic rather than obligatory. After a couple of minutes, Alex nudged her and she coughed into the mike.

'Thank you so much ... this has been a wonderful day and a sweet conclusion to a long stretch of work ... for us both. I know you will enjoy these books. Nothing like them has come out in the last thirty years ... perhaps ever. So many people are suffering in our world today and we need answers. We need answers and we need relief as well as hope ... hope that things will get better. What better chance for this than stories with answers ... real answers relevant in our world.'

She spoke on in the same vein for a few more minutes and Alex followed her briefly, warning that times would come soon wherein they would have to see drastic change if humanity was to survive.

Concerned perhaps that some might have been a little spooked by Cara's surprisingly serious speech, Carmen spoke again after Alex, concentrating more on the humorous, the touching and the exciting in these books about the Aryan people.

That evening, the key players were still celebrating at the Laughton mansion but Alex was getting tired and a growing sense of wariness hung about him. It was a great moment for them both but somehow, he felt like he was stuck in some sort of emotional no-man's land.

Everyone else was ecstatic. Nine people still laughed and chatted and drank and stood singing loudly around the Steinway grand while Cara played. During the later part of the evening, she went through at least a dozen old favourites including "Cheek to Cheek" "Camptown Races" and "Morning is Broken". Everyone sang and laughed and drank copiously, some until they were crying.

It took her a while to figure that something was wrong but in the end, when she did, she made her excuses quickly and steered Alex down to the jetty. Her father looked after the other guests.

'What are we doing here?' he asked.

'What do you mean?'

'Oh, nothing, I guess I'm just feeling like a stiff-necked old man.'

Cara had to choke back a fit of laughter, which was simply how she felt but she knew that it might not be appreciated. She could not imagine why he might be feeling that way.

'Well, you need to shake that off and you've got two choices. You can take me in the boathouse or drive the boat around to my place.'

'Just around the corner, isn't it? You lucky harbour dwellers, getting to evade the police with your fancy power boats and jetties. I think I'll have you in the boathouse.'

She smiled.

'Good choice. It's my home away from home ... when I'm not home with you.'

'Oh, so we won't be kicking over old outboard motors and the like?'

'You want me to get one in to kick?'

'Sure, why not? Got to have a spare for the fancy speedboat, don't we?'

'That has an inboard.'

'You've got me, haven't you? An answer for everything.'

She took him by the arm and they went inside. It was already lit with low lamps of various colours and there was a very comfortable looking lounge facing out over the water but Cara had other ideas and she led him up a spiral staircase into the loft, where he was unsurprised to see a big, comfortable bed.

They flopped down onto it together and held each other with that rare energy that needs no words, no kissing, no other displays of affection besides the holding itself. Cara felt special and Alex felt more relaxed so now the world outside could wait.

The morning was bright and warm and nothing felt strange to Alex anymore when he woke. Yet the innocent affection of the night before was gone and now they were hungry for each other.

It was near eleven when they finally got up and showered. When they emerged onto the porch, there was slight but not exactly small man waiting for them there — a man with straight brown hair, an easy expression and warm brown eyes. Alex suddenly felt the unease return.

'Hello. I'm Peter Armstrong. I know who you both are. I was at the book launch yesterday.'

'I didn't see you,' said Cara. 'How did you get in ... the security?'

'Your father. I asked to see him and he seemed happy to oblige.'

'Well, he must have trusted you ... but why?'

He smiled.

'Perhaps because Seria sent me. I know, he doesn't even know about her ... but I have one of these and it helps a lot.'

He showed one of the silver amulets that Seria had given them. It was unmistakeably the same.

'Yes, she has her ways, it seems,' said Alex. 'Sit down, friend, and we'll chew the fat.'

Peter grinned.

'Well, there really isn't all that much to chew ... except for that when the time comes, I'll introduce you to certain people.'

Alex felt easier then.

'When?'

'I don't know ... but I honestly think it won't be long. I know the organization and a couple of the people in it ... and it's been pretty clear to me that they're gearing up.'

'What's the organization?'

Peter sat back a little and looked from one to the other.

'Well, a lot of people are talking about them, even now, so I guess I can tell you. Have you heard of The Little River?'

'Yes,' Cara replied. 'It's in the news quite a bit. Rebels and the like. I sympathise with them.'

'So do I. Well, there's an offshoot called the Wolf Pack ... run by some people I know ... or at least they're pretty high up in it.'

'The Wolf Pack? Why is it called that?'

'I believe the leader's called Wolf.'

'You don't know him?'

'No, I haven't met him ... not yet. Quite a reputation though.'

'Is he German?'

'No. Scottish, I believe, by birth. I believe the name Wolf is ... professional.'

The unease returned.

'Oh. Do you like what they do?'

'It's hard not to. By all accounts they've helped a lot of people ... just not always by legitimate means.'

'So, he's a sort of Robin Hood.'

'You could say that.'

'They've strung up a few fellows like him.'

'I know. Anyone doing that sort of work is pretty brave in my books.'

Cara leaned forward towards Peter.

'How does he do it then? How does he get away with doing that when they've hunted down others like him?' she asked.

'I don't know ... but I do know my friends are damn good at what they do ... and they're wealthy ... at least one of them is.'

'That would help. And it makes him all the more admirable. Who would give up so much privilege to put themselves in danger helping others?'

'I think they're all a bit like that. It's what sets them apart ... and what brings them together.'

Alex got up and went to stand against the jetty railing.

'Well, I suppose it's a good thing you're here then ... but what exactly is your role in all this?'

Peter stood up as well and moved closer to him — about halfway to the railing.

'I don't know, really, except that Seria told me we should get to know each other over the next few months. I do know these people in the Wolf Pack but I have to say that they've been pretty cagey about what they do so far. I don't really know how we'll fit in to be honest but I wouldn't be surprised if our Seria had something clever up her sleeve.'

'Well, let's just enjoy,' said Alex. 'Sounds like easy work, so far. We'll get on with becoming famous and you ... what do you do?'

'I solve problems for businesses. You know, efficiency black holes, poor training, employee relations customer relations ... that sort of thing. Like you ... easy work and I pretty much set my own hours ... except if there's an emergency.'

'Do you get many of those?' Cara asked.

'Well, yes actually ... nowadays. Plenty of businesses with horror challenges. God, we can travel to Mars but a good many of us can't even retrieve a lost file on a computer.'

'Good with that sort of thing, are you?'

'Yes, very.'

'We'll have to watch him,' Alex said to Cara with a grin. 'He might just sniff out our secrets.'

'What secrets?'

'You know, where we hid the brandy.'

'Oh, yes, the brandy.'

Peter shook his head.

'Come to think of it, I could help in hiding the brandy. You'll have a lot of people interested in it after today, I can tell you. I spent all last night reading your first book ... what's it called, A New Star Ascends? I've spent a lot of time analysing functional systems and there's way too much in that book for it to be fiction.

And I peeked ahead a little. Thor ... with an all-time smacker of a spaceship.'

'You bought the full set?'

'Of course.'

'You're doing alright then. That would have been an even thousand dollars.'

'Just for a bunch of books.'

'Yes, just for a bunch of books. Still, with Thor travelling to Earth aka Midgard in flashy spaceships and building a thriving civilisation here, one would have to ask where such information might have come from. Seems there was a bunch of NASA files go missing not so very long ago. And now, first day after release, within a few hours ... maybe even a few minutes, you're going to start getting phone calls.'

Cara shot up.

'The phones. We switched them off!'

'Of course you did. Don't switch them back on just yet. Just hear me out. I won't be long, I promise. If you have anything that might compromise you, give it to me now and I'll hide it.'

'Not sure why I'd do that,' said Alex.

'So, you are the primary author.'

Alex was suddenly angry. A good many feelings about all this were still unresolved.

'You little ...!'

Peter shook his head.

'Don't be upset. You've come up with a story and it's not bad but that's the sort of shenanigans you'll be up against soon enough. If the story doesn't hold water and you can't stick to your facts as you've stated them, you'll find yourselves in all sorts of trouble.'

'Yes, I see what you mean.'

'So, is there anything that ties you to those NASA files?'

'No. Not in our possession or on any property we own.'

'Then it's probably okay ... but the minute you detect or have a problem, let me know. Is it true, by the way?'

'What?'

'That the stories were all etched on gold sheets in another language.'

Alex nodded.

'It makes you wonder, doesn't it?' he said.

Peter gave Alex his card then went to Cara and gave her one as well.

'It says, Hal Corben. Who's he?'

'Me ... but if you get into any trouble with the authorities I won't want them sniffing around me.'

'They could trace you through the number.'

'No, they couldn't. Just remember, enter three hashes before it when you call. If you don't it'll just give you a 'this phone is no longer connected' message.'

'That's one problem solved already ... but we'd like to know how we can get money to The Little River.'

'Easy one that. It is a listed charity. I'll fix it up if you like. How much?'

'Ten thousand a month?'

'That'll help a lot of people.'

Just then there was a commotion outside and with a lot of raised voices and general clamour.

'There they are already. Time to face the music.'

Alex looked at Peter sharply.

'You'll need to get away unseen.'

'Might be better ... but I'll just go and have lunch with Laughton. Already arranged ... and I'll slip away once you folk have gone off to deal with your bit of mayhem.'

Out the back, security had the crowd at bay behind the gates and were in the process of arranging a stepladder to mount the fence and talk to the crowd. Alex put his head over and found that there was a narrow walkway along the top of the wall on this side of a final level of glass. The glass was about a metre and a half high, had no grip and was sharp enough at the top to discourage gripping it. Old man Laughton had really gone to town on his security.

Outside, there were press men and women, cameras, crowds of onlookers chatting to each other and a collection of tough looking men dressed in dark grey. A great many vehicles were parked all over the place and a good many of them were an anonymous looking dark grey as well. He climbed down again.

'What do they want?' Cara asked.

'Beats me ... other than to quiz us about our sources I suppose.'

'Will you talk to them?'

'Sure. It'll help publicity.'

'I don't think we're going to need much of that.'

'Still the questions need to be answered ... or not answered as the case may be.'

Laughton's security chief was standing close by.

'You're not thinking of going out there are you?' he asked.

'I was.'

'Talk from up on the wall ... at the house end there's a wider space and a security door into the house. Do it from there and we can keep an eye on things outside while you say what you've got to say. I've got four guys at good vantage points.'

'Okay, show us to this door and we'll do it the easy way. It might look better as well.'

By the time the three of them were out on the mini balcony at the house end of the wall, a half dozen police cars had arrived as well and were trying to clear the road, despite the fact that it was a cul-de-sac and led nowhere.

Alex called out to them sharply.

'Let them be, officers. You down there, stand back and we'll get this under control.'

The officers stood still, waiting then with the rest.

'Very well, I think we can clear this all up in a few minutes. You there, with the hat, what's on your mind?'

'Did you write 'The Reign of the Dragon stories, sir?' the woman asked.

'No, I helped edit them.'

'Could we talk to the writer?' a dozen voices clamoured.

Cara stood forth.

'What do you want?' she asked.

Another clamour then one strong male voice pealed out:

'Where did you get the material?'

'I've talked about that ... at the book release. If you think there's more to it, would I tell you?'

There was an uproar.

'That mightn't have been wise,' Alex told her quietly. 'Tell them you will tell them ... then give them something. Maybe just say it's sometimes hard to know if something comes to you simply from inspiration or from visions.'

'Hoy, hoy all you down there, quiet,' yelled Carter, Laughton's security chief.

'Thank you,' said Cara when the noise subsided, 'writing's a strange business at the best of times. Most of you won't know what it's like to write a novel let alone immerse yourself for the sort of time it takes to write thirteen stories ... and a guide. Strange things happen along the way. You have dreams and sometimes they seem to go on even when you've woken up. Thoughts come to you in moments of stillness and sometimes it's hard to even remember where an idea came from.'

'How many years did it take you?' a female voice asked. 'Cat Sloane from Out There, dear.'

'A decade Cat. Around a decade.'

'You started writing these when you were sixteen? There's so much background and depth. Who are you?'

'Well, some of you must know that my father has headed up businesses around the world and I have seen a lot of things but yes, when it came to the final polish, that's where Alex came in. He's a writer of long standing and great professional strength.'

'And you married him as well.'

'I've long admired his way with words,' Cara replied, turning to smile at him.

'Is that enough to make a person marry someone?'

'Damn well should be,' Alex responded. 'Would you choose a cobbler to fix your shoes, people? Would you go to the bank for money? Words are life, ladies and gentlemen. They're everything. Damn it, you people should know that!'

After another ten minutes or so of banter and tough talk, Alex had them eating out of the palm of his hand and most packed up their equipment to leave when they disappeared from the balcony overlooking the road. Yet the police teams remained along with the men in dark grey and Laughton's security men kept an eye on their every move. Only when everyone else had left, one of the men in dark grey started to speak with the senior police officer, a sergeant, and continued in animated conversation for some time.

Chapter 12 — Break In

Inside, Laughton wanted to speak to them.

'Don't know if you know what you're dealing with here,' he told them.

'It'll blow over,' Cara reassured him.

'No, love, that's not what I'm talking about. It's those men in grey that I'm talking about. They're intel and they're not here to hear your public statements.'

'How do you know?'

'Carter told me they were speaking to the police after all the others left. One of his fellers had a directional mike set up and the boss one told the police sergeant they had orders to watch your every move ... and that the police were to cooperate.'

'So, it's started, already,' said Alex.

'Now I'm thinking I want to go home and see if everything's alright,' said Cara.

'Take Carter and one of his men with you ... on the boat ... and do it now before they send a flotilla in from that direction. I don't know what you've gone and done with all this but I can make an educated guess and I'm with you both all the way.'

Cara met her father's eyes then in a moment of deep emotional insight and knew that despite all his faults, he was a good man.

'Thank you, dad. We're right on this ... what we're doing ... and so are you.'

'Then let's not have them get the better of you.'

'No.'

Both Cara and Alex had boat licences for obvious reasons but he needed his less than she might, so he took the wheel. It was brute of a machine, a jetboat with a tuned 427 Chev engine and he wondered if he would need to use the muscle today.

Cara's unit block was only a couple of bays around but there were some suspicious-looking craft hanging around out there. He started the motor and it rumbled ominously but when Cara threw off the lines and he slipped it into reverse, it felt smooth.

'Looks like we've got company,' said Cara as a sleek looking forty-footer headed towards them.

'No speed limit here is there?'

'Not after you get thirty metres out. Until then four knots.'

'Glad you reminded me.'

'They do police it on the harbour.'

Once he was clear, Alex opened it up. It was pretty flat this afternoon and the boat took what waves there were pretty well so he roared past the bigger boat and headed out around Shark Island to the north then headed back down towards the Harbour Bridge, veering into the southern end of Rose Bay only when he was sure they had lost the following boat.

They slipped quietly into the jetty after making that big circle and tied her up, thinking all the trouble was behind them but when they got up to the fifth floor and came to Cara's front door, it was open. Alex saw a number of police inside and pulled Cara up close beside him.

'What's going on here officer?' he said addressing the nearest constable.

'You the owner?'

'No, Cara, here, is. What's happened?'

'Break in. We're finger printing the place.'

'You do that for every break in?'

'Don't even attend, usually,' the constable said with a laugh. 'Your girlfriend's pretty high profile, huh?'

Alex glared at him.

'Wife, sonny. Get me the senior officer.'

The constable left and soon came back with a sergeant.

'Sergeant John Anderson, Mr Jamieson. We were alerted by neighbours when the door was broken in and the alarm went off ... only briefly. She reported her neighbour's occupation and current profile. The decision was made to come and investigate.'

'What have you found?'

'Bit of a mess. Figured they were in a hurry. Any idea what they might be looking for?'

'Money, valuables. There wouldn't be much else.'

'I do keep a bit of cash,' Cara volunteered.

'Where?'

'In the potato bin.'

'That's a new one. Under the sink?'

'Yes.'

'Check it out constable.'

The young constable returned in a few minutes.

'Looks like near ten grand, here.'

'You're lucky,' said the sergeant. 'What's with the money?'

'Nothing. I just collect the old notes.'

The sergeant handed her the small zipped bag.

'That would be about the right amount for what you had in there?'

'Yes, about that.'

The sergeant looked at her hard.

'Ms Jamieson, there's something they wanted. Would it be about your books? A lot has been said ...'

'I know. It's just the PR machine at work Sergeant Anderson. And the books ... they are unusual.'

'Yes, from what I've heard. Your dreamed it all? Wish I had dreams like that.'

'You need a little more time on your hands, sergeant.'

'Something I don't have. What I do have is a government adviser, here, Riggs, who'd like to have a word to you both ... down at the station if you don't mind.'

'What do you mean? What possible motive could you have for inconveniencing us further?' Alex demanded.

'Damn, sir, if you don't mind my saying ... but you could be in danger. Pretty brutal what they did to the door. Riggs just wants you to know how serious this is and work out a plan to keep you safe.'

Alex glanced at Cara then and it seemed like she wanted to play along.

'Okay ... that seems like a fair thing ... but until we can arrange extra security, we can stay at Cara's father's place. He has dedicated security staff.'

'Very well, but the bigger picture, you know ... let's just see where it takes us.'

The station was Double Bay, as it happened, not far from the Laughton mansion but Riggs was hard nosed and persistent. He wanted to know every detail he could about their relationship and their situation. Alex began to wonder if he did not have another agenda.

'This business of dreaming the events of a series of thirteen novels doesn't wash with me, Jamieson,' he said towards the end, 'and it won't wash with a good many others.'

'That's not our affair,' Alex replied with easy confidence but with no warmth. 'What you believe is your business and frankly we don't give a damn.'

Riggs knew it was over before he wanted to acknowledge it with the answers petering out to bare monosyllables in the end and he knew that he could not hold them so he got up and called in a constable.

They were escorted to the garage, where the constable took them to his wagon, a Landcruiser, and returned them to the unit block so they could take the speedboat back to Laughton's.

'You know you could have called me, don't you?' said Laughton when they returned and told him the story.

'I would have been straight in contact with Connaughton and he'd have had you out in minutes.'

'It doesn't matter,' Cara replied. 'It's not like they were holding us on suspicion or anything. Technically, as they said, they were just trying to protect us.'

'Not damn likely. Trying to nose in for sure. Keep them well out of it, I say.'

'Which we will,' said Alex. 'We're going to head back down to Eucumbene in the morning and get right away from this shit.'

'Not a bad idea ... but what have you got in the way of security down there?'

'Just a bunch of friendly, nosy neighbours and a pig gun.'

'Got them, have you?'

'Just a few.'

Grant could see that Alex was angry.

'Well relax for now and have a drink. We'll see what auntie has to say about today's events, if anything. Gin isn't it?'

'Mostly. Like absinth, it's good for the artists' creative juices.'

'I'll steer clear of both. Good old Scotch for me.'

Several channels of the TV news had them on as the headline story.

'Extraordinary events in Sydney's east today as crowds gathered outside the Laughton family mansion to see Australia's newest literary sensations. Rumours of missing government files in the US state of Florida abound and tally with the release of what is tipped to be a worldwide literary smash hit. The authoress, Cara Jamieson and her husband spoke with media and police outside her father's Double Bay home only to later discover that Ms Jamieson's Rose Bay unit had been broken into.'

Somehow, they had got footage of Cara and Alex in the speeding jetboat as they were headed for Rose Bay in the early afternoon and the whole affair seemed to be taking on a distinctly spy flavoured aura. They were such a spectacular couple and the media loved it of course, most of their journalists spending much of their life bored witless as they did.

'Should trade in the E type for an old Aston Martin DB5, my boy,' laughed Laughton, mellowed somewhat now by his second whisky.

'James Bond never had it so good,' said Cara, snuggling up to Alex and thinking that her husband had a good deal of the debonair about him.

'James Bond never had a wife.'

'Yes, he did ... for a few hours.'

'Until they shot her. Heaven forbid.'

All this talk should have made Alex feel pumped up but somehow it failed to. In fact, it made him more aware of his deficiencies. Would he act like Bond if he needed to? Would he ever get to the heart of any matter — or deal with killing someone if he had to?

'I'm thinking that you did get those NASA files they're talking about ... somehow,' Laughton said unexpectedly.

Alex's heart skipped a beat.

'Now, Grant, you've got to know we can't say anything about that,' he said, instantly defensive, 'but if you want reassurance that we're doing what we're doing for the right reasons, you know that these stories have a good message for everyone ... an important message.'

'I know. I've been reading them too ... carefully, slowly ... and yes, I wouldn't see them hidden either.'

'Then you're okay with all this?'

'Better than okay. I'll do anything I can to help. You know that.'

'No, I didn't really ... but it's good to know.'

'Never really was one for god, myself. He seems to have abandoned the human race ... if he was ever really there in the first place ... but a completely different picture emerges from these books, doesn't it?'

'Yes, it's astonishing, really. Not that I don't believe in a creator god but it's a big universe and I don't think such a powerful being would be obsessed with riding herd on us.'

'Totally. You got it and this is all worth it. I couldn't be prouder of my daughter ... for all sorts of reasons ... but I don't know who could really come up with this sort of stuff without some sort of inspiration at the very least ... and there you are ... these files went missing from NASA ... an official murdered for them. It had to be important. Well, now we know exactly what was that important and it's flooding yours and Cara's bank accounts with wonderful, beautiful dollars. It's marvellous really. I just hope you can keep riding the wave cause one that size can dump awfully hard.'

It was true. Alex looked at his father-in-law with renewed appreciation. He did have good sense and might well prove to be a useful ally.

Chapter 13 — NASA Homes In

Sales after the first week began to rocket, not just in Australia but around the world. Many countries were beginning to be hard hit by the resurging corona viruses taking new and strange forms and people desperately needed some sort of relief from the daily tyranny of their lives. This for millions now took the form of escape ... into the world of Arya.

Well before Christmas it became clear that Alex and Cara would soon be millionaires many times over, even with the ten times currency reset that had happened in the late thirties. They had shared the funds equally by early agreement and back down in the Snowies, for a number of reasons other than money, they were the wonder of their quiet rural neighbourhood. It should have eased Alex's self doubts and it did but only at a superficial level. In the end, money might not make much difference at all — unless the right things were done with it.

Even the local youngsters and teenagers were captivated by the drama of their fame and fortune — and given that, they respected Alex the more for his going out in his old Hilux ute like everyone else around the locality to cut firewood when he needed it.

The first signs of winter came early that season with a series of strong south west changes rolling through by early April and the woodheap was sparse so on the first calm day, Saturday the seventh, Alex and Cara went up the hill to a bit of forest that had been burned out many years ago. Thousands of tall dead trees still stood up there, and Alex felled one every so often, as did most of his neighbours. They cut it, threw it onto the ute tray and were setting out to return down the hill when a chopper raced over the lake and up the hill towards them.

The storm grey machine flew over, banked and descended down towards the Teahouse Hill landing area and unexpectedly, Alex knew just what to do.

'What's going on?' Cara asked as they set out down the rough track.

'Don't ask me how I know but I think this could be some sort of delegation.'

'Ben and the others will be right onto them if they land in the Cove.'

'Good, then we'll give them some time to learn what's what. No need to rush down there with a full load of wood on.'

Down on Teahouse Hill, which no longer sported a teahouse courtesy of it being burned out in the nineties, the locals had already surrounded the chopper with rifles drawn. Sensibly, the pilot kept the rotors running for a while but when it looked like tempers had cooled, he started the shut down. It was just about then that Alex and Cara arrived.

'We only want to talk to Alex Jamieson!' called out a sandy-haired man in the front passenger seat.

'He's coming now,' Ben replied, bushy red beard swaying with the energy of his assertion. 'Only one of you out at a time. The rest of you can stay put.'

A taller man with a dark blue polo sweater and jeans jumped out and strolled over confidently.

'Mike Carsen, chief negotiator,' he said to Ben just as Alex jumped out of the ute.

'Don't care who you are mate. Hands up and spread your legs.'

'I'm just a NASA scientist buddy. You don't need to pat me down.'

Carsen had a deep mellow voice, the sort of voice you could trust.

'And you don't need to talk.'

Ben held onto him with an iron grip and shook him for a few seconds, just so he would be sure who was boss.

Alex and Cara looked on with barely veiled amusement and not a little satisfaction.

'Thanks Ben,' said Alex, 'but I'm pretty sure this one only wants to talk. Keep me covered though.'

'Sure, mate. Take care with these bastards though. Bloody yanks.'

'I'll take this one for a little walk down by the lake edge. If you wouldn't mind following within buckshot range, that'd be great.'

'No worries.'

Alex nodded to the tall dark-haired guy sporting a crew cut and half-rims over steely blue eyes and began to walk. The fellow half ran to catch up. They walked down the stone steps and nearly all the way across the dam wall before Alex spoke.

'So, what do you want?' he asked.

'We want answers. You can't have got all that detail from your girlfriend's dreams. We already had the gist of it when Sarah Hilton gave her report the day she went missing. Sure, we hadn't read it in its entirety but the gist was a dead ringer for what's in your novels.'

Alex stopped for a moment and met Carsen's eyes. It was a positive development — good news. Now, for the first time, he felt certainty almost on every level; strategically, emotionally and intellectually.

'You didn't have any backup copies,' he said speculatively. 'No, that's it, she must have wiped them ... disposed of them before she left the office that day. She was going to steal what you had. Still doesn't mean we found what you lost.'

'It couldn't be otherwise. Too much of a coincidence. You and I both know that sort of thing just doesn't happen. And yes, good guess ... we don't have any copies ... but when the rover transceiver gets back online we'll get it to send the data again.'

'Why is it offline?'

'We don't know. Some sort of fault. Receives but doesn't send. It's getting old but there's a new one planned for next year.'

'Next year eh? So, you really can't prove anything ... and by next year, who knows what?'

They started walking again and Alex took Carsen down a rough winding path towards the waters edge, dodging the occasional rocky outcrop and feeling ever more confident. It reassured him, as well, that Carsen was so obliging.

'The thing is, we know about your missing twin brother. We know that someone using his passport was in Florida at the time of the abduction and flew out back to Australia the day after. He still hasn't shown up so we have to assume it was you. If it was you, we could have you arrested and extradited at the very least for travelling under a false passport.'

Alex grinned.

'Brave try, friend, but you don't know where he is and you'd never be able to prove I was the twin who travelled to the US. So there's no point in trying these push 'n shove routines. Wasn't born yesterday.'

'Okay but you must know that if any of this was ever proved, you could do time. The thing is, we could keep that from happening.'

'Why? What could I do for you in return?'

Carsen smiled wryly.

'Not much really. We can read the books now like anyone else, and I take it you haven't changed much.'

'If I was working with someone else's stuff, I might well change a few stylistic things. This character, Thor, is a unique philosopher and to put a stop to that angle would be the last thing on my mind.'

'Well, that's the thing. Some of us feel the same way and think you did the right thing. You have a sympathy with him that serves us all well.'

Alex turned back to face him directly.

'I didn't expect you to say that.'

'We're human too.'

'Some of you.'

'I'll second that. Some of the people we deal with every day scarcely qualify.'

Down near the water's edge now — and it was low given that there had not been a great deal of rain recently — they looked out across the water towards Hallstrom Island.

'Then I'd be scared for you ... talking to me like this,' Alex said, quietly.

'Dammit, I'm authorised.'

'But are you authorised to negotiate like this?'

'Our conversation is not being recorded.'

'As far as you know.'

'Yes.'

'Well, in any case, I agree with you. I believe I do have something I can offer you.'

'What?'

'Well, it's bloody obvious, doesn't it? There's six books missing ... this Rings of Fate group.'

'Yes, the ones supposedly from our prehistoric past. We've searched everywhere ... even in other nearby lava tubes. There are no more books.'

'Really? I hardly think these godlike beings would just forget to put in place a big part of a history they wished to preserve.'

'But they did, apparently.'

'Well, as I said, I think I could provide some insight into this ... so if you can, set us up a meeting with your top brass ... in Sydney. And tell them not to give me any shit or we'll be out of there so fast you'll be reaching for the light switch.'

Carsen nodded.

'I understand. I'm sure I'd feel the same way. In a week's time?'

'Fine ... let's knock on some brass and see if we can't get a ring out of it.'

Carson grinned.

'Nice. I'll see to it and we'll be in touch.'

'Great ... back to work then.'

'Nice little place here ... but don't you get bored?'

'We creative types never get bored, sonny ... just emotional. Too much noise plays merry hell with the thoughts.'

'You're operating on another level.'

Alex detected admiration beneath the overt surprise.

'Yeah, who knows, maybe my own writings will get a look-in one day.'

Carsen's eyebrows lifted.

'I never thought of that. What sort of stuff do you normally write?'

'Adventure thrillers with a hint of sci-fi ... speculating on the alien invasion theme ... but with the difference that the invasion happened a long time ago ... not just last week.'

Carsen nodded.

'You wouldn't believe the rumours that get around HQ.'

'Maybe one day we'll talk some more.'

Strangely, Alex did not feel so angry anymore.

The lanky American ran back to the chopper. It lifted off and then they were gone. Curious now, the locals crowded around — twelve or thirteen of them and Ben approached.

'Everything alright, Alex?'

'Yeah, I think they might be coming to their senses.'

'That'll be the day!'

Cara was about as hopeful as Ben, knowing well how things operated in higher circles.

'Do you really think you should meet with these US bureaucrats?' she asked him later when they were seated by the fire together after dinner. 'You'll be going into the lion's den for sure.'

'Maybe ... but not unarmed. It's all pretty much in the open and I think I can trust that Carsen fellow. He doesn't seem too against the idea that we came up with these tales independently. And I know now that they can't prove otherwise. Apparently, they don't have any of the original files ... and the rover's broken down. To do him justice, he didn't have to tell me that. They actually seem to need our help. Whatever we've got to offer, it could be worth playing along. I can't see the harm in it. These other stories must be somewhere but the truth is, we don't stand much of a chance of finding them without these flunkies.'

'What's your angle?'

'I didn't tell him ... but y' know, I think I get how Thor thinks and I don't believe he would do the same thing twice. It just doesn't make sense. I mean the gold leafed books are something ... a teaser but he didn't need to do all the books that way ... and even if he did, maybe he wouldn't even place them on the same planet. Yes, he'd keep us guessing.'

'Their society does seem pretty high tech.'

'Yeah, he ... or the narrator if it isn't him, actually mentioned several times that they have data storage devices. Why wouldn't they use them?'

'Don't they think he did?'

'This Mike guy made no mention of it. I know how they think, these bureaucratic types. Just what's there in front of their eyes. No sense for the overall picture.'

'So, you'll go into your meeting with them armed ... armed with a theory!'

'Yes, and they'll want as much as they can get ... before they realize it might not actually be in their interests to find it. Half of these guys wouldn't even realize the significance of the Aryan take on life until it was too late for them to hide it.'

'Probably not. If and when they do, expect trouble.'

Alex nodded.

'I'm pretty sure we can out manoeuvre them.'

'Maybe we can ... but do you think you should consult Seria over this?'

Alex thought for a moment.

'No ... she was all good with this ... the books being released ... culture changing. I think she has other priorities and I don't think this will bother her.'

'Good, then I guess we get to relax for a few days before heading back up to Sinney, the Sinful City.'

'Guess so.'

Chapter 14 — The Summit

The call came only two days later. The brass would see them in Sydney over lunch two days hence, Wednesday the eleventh. Cara had always had a thing for the Summit Restaurant so they arranged to meet the NASA nobs there over a long lunch.

'No getting away from that place in a hurry if there's trouble, though,' she said when Alex told her.

'If they interrupt the lunch with some sort of woe I'll tip them over the side.'

'Okay. Very public place too, so maybe they couldn't do much.'

There were three who met them at the table and Laughton had suggested that his lawyer, Frank Connaughton, should accompany them. Alex was confident they wanted his cooperation but their having a good lawyer could keep things fair.

'Just the sort of place for us,' said the nearest, a familiar face.

'Nice to see you again, Mike,' said Cara.

'Pleasure's mine. This is Joe and Aden. Joe Miller's my immediate boss and Aden is one of those professional negotiator people.'

'Not much point in him if you tip us off like that,' Alex observed.

'No, that's the point. We want you to know we're being up front, even if our organization does dictate who comes along.'

'That all sounds fine and rosy but do the top brass really want to be up front?'

'Top brass sent us Joe because he's up there with them.'

'Then it has to be alright.'

'Sure it does.'

Alex laughed.

'They may have you more conned than us.'

'Could be. Anyway, here's the menu. We'll have the best with a story or two thrown in.'

The place was not busy but well-attended. After ordering, the six at the table began to eye each other off a little more seriously.

'When we last spoke,' Mike began, 'you talked about the missing books ... as if you knew just what would be the trick.'

Alex shook his head.

'You're being hopeful ... but truth is, I did have something in mind. Naturally you assumed you might have missed something but I'm thinking you didn't think through what *sort* of thing that might be ... you know, that it might take a different form.'

Mike glanced at Joe and they both nodded.

'We didn't really sit down and brainstorm it,' Joe admitted, 'but we did do a bunch of scans and searches.'

'Just what I thought.'

Cara felt sorry for them for a moment and met Joe's eye with the hint of a smile.

'It's the prerogative of the creative writer,' she said, 'to think of things others might not ... to think of alternatives out of the ordinary.'

'Yes, I suppose so.'

'You don't sound very convinced,' said Alex, 'but you're in for a surprise.'

'Maybe there was something else in the original material ... some sort of advice about where to look,' said Joe, accusingly.

Alex was not impressed.

'You just don't want to believe in the unique worth of the creative mind, do you?'

'No ... no, of course we need creative minds. I mean it'd be pretty boring if we didn't have any reading ... any entertainment.'

Alex grinned, a little dourly.

'Ah, yes, we can't do without the court jester. But I'm more than that. Fact is I'm really going to throw you in this and beat you at your own game. Ever heard of the concept of the hunch?'

'Of course. About where or how the rest of the material might be hidden?'

'Yes ... but dy' really understand what a hunch is?'

'Gut feeling.'

'Yes but it doesn't just come from nowhere and there are so many accounts of how hunches have saved the day ... even saved peoples' lives. The best concept of it is that the individual with the hunch really does know it's right.'

'Then what about it?'

'We need an agreement first. What I've got to tell you is pretty simple so there won't be any hidden layers ... and I won't have you dudding me because on paper it's so simple.'

Joe's pallid face clouded with sudden anger. Entering middle age and itching for a fight, Alex thought. Just the type to fire up quickly.

'Dammit, we're the ones who've been dudded. It's our material.'

Alex leaned forward, feeling bullish.

'No it wasn't. That's just where you're wrong. It's not yours. It's Thor's ... and I believe he will have hidden it in a way that might be clearer to somebody who understood him a little better ... who sympathised with his goals and his motives.'

'You seem very sure of yourself.'

'You forget how we got hold of this material.'

'You mean how you say you got hold of it.'

'Whatever. The fact is, you seem a bit contentious now. Do you really want my input?'

Joe's gaunt face fell.

'I didn't mean it to come off that way,' he said. 'It's just that it rankles to have had this then have it slip through our fingers.'

'I wouldn't look at it that way. Mike understands. Your top brass would never have let you see it anyway. This Sarah Hilton lady at NASA ... pretty well guarded, wasn't she?'

'Until the afternoon she went missing and the tag vehicle broke down unexpectedly.'

'What was it, just out of interest?'

'Faulty radiator hose. They didn't notice until the motor was pretty well cooked.'

'Mustn't have called her to get her to be extra careful, either.'

'Caught up in the moment, I guess. Young agents. They're always too cocky.'

'True ... but what you don't seem to realize is that all it would have taken was a small stab from a fid or a needle to sabotage that radiator hose.'

'Maybe.'

'So, process this ... if things hadn't happened the way they did, you might never have even heard of this ... nor got to read the books. I mean would you have read them at all if you didn't think they came from a lava tube on Mars? Do you normally read sci-fi or fantasy? You have read them, haven't you?'

Mike Carsen answered that.

'Of course. They are astonishing and yes, I wouldn't want to have not known about them. It's a different sort of take on things.'

'Good. Now we're getting somewhere. Do you want to know my theory?'

Mike glanced at Joe then back to Alex.

'Yes, that's why we're here.'

'Then listen well. I want exclusive rights to publish those books as well. I mean, it only makes sense, doesn't it? You've got to understand that we can't have the source jumping all over the place, right?'

'Aren't you making enough money already?'

'Yes, and it's not about the money anymore. It's nice to have it but we're headed for billions of dollars in royalties just from Reign.'

'Then why do you want more?'

'Well, the US government doesn't need it and can't really admit to these books coming from a lava tube on Mars anyway. But if you want, we could agree to donate the bulk of the revenue from the rest to charity ... as long as it's a charity of our own choosing.'

'Yes, a charitable foundation. I think it much more likely the top brass would agree to that. Some of them don't like how much you're making.'

'Then you'll agree?'

'Do you want anything else?'

'Immunity from further enquiry or prosecution of any kind.'

'Yes.'

'I also want your top brass to consider coming clean about their own Mars material at some stage. It wouldn't hurt us ... only add weight to our position.'

'I'm not sure about that.'

'Well, you just think about what all this means. You guys say that the material Cara dreamed up is virtually identical to what was found in a lava tube on Mars ... apparently left there by one Thor from the distant planet Arya. You've read the books and in particular, you must see the merits of us owning the philosophies specified in Peace of the Hammer ... but also in many passages in the other books.'

'Interesting. I think some would call them ... radical.'

'And they'd be right, if they knew the true meaning of that word ... of the root ... in other words the true understanding of the matter. I mean, the roots of trees match their leaves, do they not?'

'A very apt metaphor ... when dealing with matters of Norse gods.'

'Yes. Very apt and very true. If you or anyone truly wants a better world, they will want these books to be read, to be appreciated and celebrated ... and to be understood as the truth ... the truth of our ancient forebears.'

Joe looked impressed.

'You do make a good case. As it happens, I am authorised, if it seems likely that your line of enquiry seems promising, to agree to the sorts of requests you've specified.'

Alex took a good slug of the Apple Thief pink lady cider he was drinking and sighed, not altogether sure that anything or anyone from NASA would remain true to itself or themselves.

'Okay. Then talk to my lawyer.'

'Who?'

'He's right here. Frank is my lawyer. I know he doesn't look like one but in fact he's a very good one.'

Frank grinned and pushed forward a surprisingly slender document — only three pages in all.

'It's all there, gentlemen. I'll have all three of you sign it, you Joe as primary signatory and the others as witnesses. Then we can talk.'

Joe hesitated, no more than a split second, and Alex knew then that there would be trouble. Even so, it might shake out well in the end.

'Very well.'

The three signed the document then looked up expectantly at Alex.

'I did tell you it would be simple,' he warned them. 'The thing is, we know that Thor had dealt with all sorts of establishment types all his life. He knew that in any society they would tend have too much control. So, his solution to security would be off-beat, imaginative and not a little sneaky, as I see it.'

'Yes.'

'Sneaky but simple. Some sort of signal to open something or release something ... perhaps switch it on.'

'A key,' said Mike.

'Yes, a key ... something real but invisible is my guess. Something like ...'

'Ultra-violet.'

'Or infra red ... switching on some device that you'd never see otherwise no matter how hard you searched. Personally, I'd pick infra-red. Thor had a great love of fire and the spiritual vigour it represented. Do you have any way of producing it on Mars?'

'Yes, we do ... UV and infra. Sometimes we need to warm things so the robotic device is equipped ...'

'What about that fault? Have you fixed it?'

'No, but we can still tell it to do stuff. It just won't send anything back to us.'

'Then it won't work.'

'It might. We don't know what will happen. If the vault is designed to be activated by a signal, it might have the capacity to send one as well.'

'Then you could have your solution and Cara and I might see these texts within a week or so.'

'Yes, of course, but you don't know how slow bureaucracy works. A month, maybe. We must go now and see to this!'

Alex frowned.

'But the food's just arriving. Here's the waitress now.'

'So it is. Maybe we can spare a moment for a taste but we really should get going. More for you three I guess ... and it's on us ... but we'll have to fly back with this pronto.'

'Then you like the idea?'

Carsen nodded.

'Wouldn't have thought of it myself.'

'Nor I,' said Joe and Aden at once.

'It's that creative flair,' Cara observed.

'Yes, you got us there.'

The NASA guys took a little of each dish onto their bread roll plates and ate it quickly, leaving the rest for their guests.

'Enjoy the lunch,' said Joe, standing. 'This lobster is excellent.'

Aden and Mike stood with him and in moments, they were gone.

'That was a good guess,' said Frank after they left. 'Do you really think that's it?'

'Yes, I'm sure of it. Especially now, having seen them hurry off like that.'

'Then it seems both you and Cara do have a special relationship with Thor.'

Alex grinned.

'Maybe.'

Back at Laughton's mansion, they found him at home and had an early evening drink with him.

'You look smug,' he observed, looking hard at Alex.

'Yes, maybe I do. Things are going better than I ever thought they would ... but I'm not really sure if it's NASA I'm dealing with or the CIA. One moment I feel safe and the next I'm not so sure.'

'Don't alarm yourself. They're all like that ... bureaucrats everywhere. They don't truly know what they want so they're always looking for the brilliant success story no matter what the cost.'

'I won't argue with you there. I've seen it dozens of times ... no probably a lot more than that ... but somehow this is different.'

Laughton patted his daughter on the cheek, fondly.

'It's bigger,' he said.

'Than anything I've seen before?'

'Yes.'

'I know that in a way it is ... with more yet to come ... but why do you say so?'

'Haven't you seen the papers today? The TV, the radio, the internet ... what ever you like to name, they're talking about the Time Vault saga. They're so frantic I don't think half of them have been to sleep.'

'Could do with some myself.'

'Not so quick, son. I don't know if you really appreciate how serious this is. No, I didn't think so. Well, did you know that I have an arms cabinet?'

'I know you've got security and that they have weapons.'

'Well, there's three on at night and there's still plenty of ways you could get into this place if you tried.'

'As long as you came by chopper.'

'Ha. Water, over the gate, over the fence. I'm not going to be caught out by some sneak attack. I've a handgun going under the pillow and a shotgun by my bed. I want you to do the same. You're protecting my daughter as well, you know.'

'I don't think it's come to that,' said Cara. 'Maybe one day it will ... but not yet.'

'Just be careful. That's all I'm saying. And did it go okay? Did you get what you wanted?'

'Yes ... we got an agreement that they'll give us the Rings series ... if they find it. I told them what to do to find it and I think it'll work.'

'If it does, do you think they'll stick by what they agreed on and give it to you?'

163

'We agreed to set up a charity to receive the proceeds.'

Laughton laughed.

'They don't really care about that. They just want to win. They want to be the ones who come out on top and be damned to hell with everyone else.'

'Yes, I believe you're right ... and it's all or nothing. If they trump us, they'll start kicking us around but if we trump them ... again ... they'll fall apart. God knows what chaos will follow a defeat ... but I think it'll be nasty, mainly for them.'

Laughton looked at his son-in-law, only ten years younger than him, curiously.

'What have you got in mind?'

'Not what ... who.'

'Someone who can help?'

'Very likely. I'll turn in, I think. Got a few things to think over.'

Laughton felt it best if they slept in the main house so Alex went upstairs to Cara's room, there, and lay down to gather his thoughts.

The lights were low and somehow, he managed to fall asleep. While he was out and while Cara was talking with her father, he had a dream about racing in a fast car towards an unknown destination.

When Cara came in, he woke in confusion and she lay down next to him, reassuring him.

'It's all getting very complex,' she said.

'I know. Tell me.'

'I feel like we have no future ... as if it's all going to end in some terrible pile-up.'

'Yes, I just had this dream ... and it was kind if like that ... like racing in a fast car to nowhere.'

'Exactly. Turn over and I'll give you a massage. You seem very tense.'

'God, you know what to do, don't you?'

She started on his neck and shoulders and worked her way down.

'We really don't know where we're going in all this, do we?' she said after a while.

'Perhaps not at the moment,' he replied, 'but I know Thor said something about this in A New Star Ascends ... about the divine's role in all this. He and Freya were talking about predestiny and he said that intellect carefully used led to a higher purpose ... so they didn't have to just accept an ignominious destiny.'

Cara sat up, excited.

'She replied by saying that she had initially imagined he was talking up predestiny merely to present the worst-case scenario.'

'Yes,' he affirmed, 'he agreed with her and put it so well. I loved that next line of his. "After all, what great story can be created without a master plan, and who would like a story unless its master plan brought it to a glorious and surprising conclusion?"'

'So ... why would anyone try so hard for the particular result they took a shine to?'

'Yes, indeed,' he agreed, 'because "the divine's conception would have to be better and if there was a higher architect, why would *his* conception of our greatest adventures be anything but brilliant?"'

'Could that actually be the ultimate expression of faith?' Cara asked.

'I think, perhaps, its highest form ... trust in the ability of the divine to reveal truth in the most amazing way possible is that.'

Alex then recalled the following passage.

'"After all, can we as limited mortal beings have anything like the complete knowledge of the universe that would allow us to set the most interesting, rewarding, best possible goals?"'

'It's refreshing,' she sighed in a contented way.

Alex grinned and raised his eyebrows slightly.

'"Why would we even acknowledge the divine, if there was nothing the divine will could do for us?"'

'Why indeed?' Cara replied. 'Things will work out in the end because we could have done nothing else better than what we did.'

'And the fate of many people might depend on us doing what we see as best rather than simply doing what we think we are expected to do,' he told her.

'Well, that's true,' she agreed. 'We didn't really take the moral high road.'

'Funny that ... but we did do the right thing. I did and you have since you came on board with it all. Just think, what we have done might well facilitate this Wolf Pack that Seria told us about. By the sounds of it, they're doing truly significant things ... protecting helpless people then building them up to be stronger so they can fight when and where necessary.'

'They must be courageous ... and anything we can do for them, we should. They're up against a rotten system.'

'You're a friend of the PM's, aren't you?'

'Dad is. Kane likes to think of me as a friend as well but I really don't like him that much. I don't think he's evil but he's one of those people who has spent too long around evil and has lost his ability to resist it.'

'You can hardly blame him. It must be difficult.'

'True ... but he's still done some unforgiveable things. Signing away our sovereign rights with these international treaties. It's irresponsible.'

Cara worked away at a difficult knot in Alex's back then exhaled at the same time as him except that his was in pain.

'Well, we're in the thick of it now,' he said.

'Yes, this Wolf Pack ... but I've also just recently heard more about The Little River. It started before the Wolf Pack and it seems to be more about just helping than helping with a price. I think we should support that as well. It's more of a social welfare cooperative ... set up for those outside the system.'

'Yeah, they give all sorts of help ... from food to legal representation. By the people for the people. Yes, we should help them too.'

'I wonder what Seria would think about that?'

'Doesn't really seem to be her game ... but I don't imagine she would disapprove.'

Not long after that, Cara flopped down beside him and switched off the bedside lamp. Within minutes, they were both asleep.

Alex slept dreamlessly for a while then suddenly there was a voice telling him to wake up. He thought he did wake up then but when he opened his eyes he saw Seria with a sort of halo behind her and nothing else.

'No, I'm not in your bedroom,' she said. 'You're still asleep but awake in a dream.'

'I feel very awake.'

'Good ... because you need to remember this. You'll be sent a special radio signal soon so you'll need to get a Compuscan short wave radio setup with its own dish and leave it set to the universal frequency scan. It'll pick up the signal and turn it into text so you can just print it out. Then you should probably get a professional translator onto the job. You could do it yourself with your uncle's program but you should have someone good check it through for the best clarity.'

'The books?'

'Yes, it's the books. NASA is going to look again, using the advice you gave them, and I'm pretty sure it will work. There's a lot of infighting going on and it might still take a few days but you'd better get that receiver tomorrow. You'll be able to use it anywhere but it would be better in the bush where there's less interference.'

'Okay, buy the ...'

'Compuscan'

'Yes, buy the Compuscan, take it down to the Cove and listen. Day and night on shifts?'

'No, it has a record function. You'll just have to fast forward through it in the morning to see what's there.'

'Okay.'

'See you.'

'See you.'

Chapter 15 — The Wolf Pack

On the morning of May the seventeenth, Alex was on the point of deciding to return home to the Cove the next day when he took a call from Peter.

'Seria wants you to meet my friends now,' he said, recognizing Alex's resonant media trained voice immediately. 'She says it's time for you to go and tell them what they need to do with the SWR.'

'Why can't you tell them?'

'I don't even know what the SWR is. Fact is, she's very hush-hush about it. Doesn't tell me much at all. I'm just the courier.'

'Aren't you worried her intentions might not be above board?'

'Not at all. I don't expect them to be. She's helped me in all sorts of ways I'd rather not go into ... but good ways in case you needed to hear that.'

'Okay, I guess that's a basis for trust.'

'Could you come tomorrow? Northern Beaches about two?'

'Where?'

'Fish and chip shop in Collaroy ... right opposite the beach.'

'Alright if Cara comes?'

'Don't see why not. See you then.'

On Friday, they took Cara's new Ineos SUV for a lower profile. On the way, a bit before midday, Alex suddenly remembered the dream with Seria that he had had during the night.

'Cara, would you mind looking up who sells a radio called a Compuscan?'

'Thought we were going to meet these people.'

'We are but there's time to spare. Might even be somewhere on the way.'

'Looks like it is. Cammeray. Miller Street.'

'Great, we're only minutes away.'

They were in fact approaching the Harbour Bridge, it's great grey arch looming overhead, and Alex took the lane for the Cammeray exit.

In a few minutes, they were outside the shop, which was small and unassuming. It gave little away on its front but within, it was clearly well-stocked with all sorts of interesting devices.

'Compuscan?' said the manager. 'Nice bit of kit. It'll receive almost any kind of signal. Don't sell a lot of them but we have two in stock at the moment. Bit on the pricey side.'

Cara and Alex smiled at each other and with that smile, the manager seemed to recognize them.

'Oh, I know you. Mr and Mrs Jamieson. Pleased to meet you. Of course, price won't be an issue with you. Will you need someone to set it up?'

'No,' Alex replied, 'my understanding is that it's portable. We'll be using it out of town but if you could give us a bit of a run down now, that would be appreciated. Do you take gold or silver?'

'Either. Absolutely. I'll give you ten percent. Not sure about portable though. It does have a battery but these things are a bit hefty. We sell a backpack for it if you plan on using it out in the open.'

Half an hour later, they had the gist of the instructions and seven thousand dollars or so in gold and silver changed hands. The manager helped them load it and by then they had barely enough time to make the two o'clock meeting, especially with the heavy traffic. Cara knew how to deal with it, though, from long experience.

'We should probably use a good translator if we do get the signal I'm hoping to get,' Alex told her while stopped at a set of lights.

'Holly could do that,' Cara replied. 'She's free lance so she could come down to the Cove with us and work on it ... hopefully at short notice. Get her on the phone now. Holly Robinson.'

'Of course. Good choice.'

Holly answered almost straight away.

'Holly? Alex Jamieson.'

'Oh, hi Alex. Nice to hear from you. You guys must have been busy since the book release.'

'Too right. Listen, we might have something new soon that will need translating or at least checking. Any chance you could work on it with us?'

'Sure. No problem.'

'It'll probably take a while and we'll be working down at my place in the Snowies.'

There was a pause.

'Go down to your place in the Snowies just before winter? When?'

'That's the trouble. We don't quite know yet and it could be tomorrow or could be weeks away.'

'That's a bit awkward but I'll try to arrange things to go as soon as possible.'

'Great. Look, it is a bit hush-hush, so just tell people it's a holiday, okay?'

'Done. I'll wait for your call.'

They made it in to Collaroy at two fifteen. There did not seem to be anyone in the fish and chip shop but then they noticed two men seated with their backs to them right at the back.

'Peter?' Alex called out.

One of the men got up. It was Peter.

'I took the liberty of ordering for you. Hope you don't mind.'

'Fish and chips? Not at all. Nice day for it too.'

'Damn cool, I say, for autumn.'

The other man stood and put out a hand.

'Good to meet you,' he said. 'We thought we might eat over on the beach. At least the sun has a bit of punch in it still ... and we can talk.'

A couple of minutes later, the steaming order came and the four headed across the road. The air was very cool but it was clear and the sun did still have some warmth.

'Sydney in the autumn is perfect, don't you think?' said Damon.

'Even on a day like this, yes.'

There were tables on the promenade and they sat down to eat. Peter made the introductions between Cara and Alex and Damon and they got down to business.

'It seems clear to us at the Wolf Pack that there's more to you two than meets the eye,' said Damon. 'You could have come across your information by chance and be making the most of it just for the money but let's face it, you're both writers, particularly you Alex. It's been your career from day one.'

'It's not just the money,' Alex replied, 'but money's nice ... and helpful.'

'We find that in the Wolf Pack, also. We support many people, mainly in and through The Little River ... and they support us ... but we do other things that require money also. You might say we deal with the seedy side of life and try not to end up seedy like it.'

'That's pretty much what we've heard,' said Cara, 'but does the Wolf Pack have any plans to get bigger?'

'It's not that simple. Training requirements are extensive and the risks are considerable. Trust, also, gets diluted amongst larger groups of people. In principle growth is a good thing, yes, but only within the practical limitations.'

'We don't want to see the world continue to degenerate,' Alex told him. 'if we can help people slow that down and maybe reverse it a bit just by throwing in a bit of money, there's no down side.'

'Well, to go to practical matters, we have particular protocols for fund raising. It's almost always staged thefts, break-ins or burglaries so no one can be tied to us.'

'Wouldn't the authorities hound you after so many unpunished crimes?'

'Police in this state don't pursue anyone unless they're pushed to and there's a lot of fees now for lodging a complaint.'

'So, the law's on your side.'

Damon laughed.

'Sure, but of course we do other things that anger them immensely. They'd love to wipe us off the face of the planet ... but we have our ways.'

'What sorts of things do you do?' Cara asked.

Damon grinned.

'Me? Nothing really. I'm not an operative ... but our people run with the gangs and destroy them from within, freeing a lot of people in the process. They do break-ins to get info that incriminates politicians and bureaucrats, and they even sanction people occasionally, when what they do is are bad enough to warrant punishment and the law ignores them. It's a complex operation but god knows, it's needed.'

'I didn't realize,' said Cara. 'Overseas, yes things are falling apart ... but here?'

'The police protect the wealthy areas more than anything else now. Nothing much is done outside them. You've been sheltered.'

'Yes, I suppose I have ... but my husband has lived for quite a while in the country.'

'Things are definitely more down to earth there. Something bad happens, there are consequences for the actor. Folk in the sticks have always had a way of looking after each other.'

'A little bit,' Alex agreed. 'Well, we're happy to help out with the funding but there may be something else we can do too.'

Damon looked interested.

'Yes?'

'I've been made aware of a Scottish organization that you should look into. From what I understand, they could be of some assistance in your cause. I've been told that you should listen for them on short wave radio and they go by the name of Zephyr.'

'Who told you about them?' Damon asked.

'That I can't tell you, for the time being ... but as I understand it, these people have supported you where they could, anonymously, already.'

'I see. Zephyr. This does surprise me ... yet I know I shouldn't be. You people seem to have a knack for digging up information.'

'I am a free lance journalist and have been for nearly all of my working life. That's what a good journo does ... digs up info.'

'Of course.'

'And it seems to get stranger and stranger. I can't vouch for what we're dealing with here but you could be in for a few more surprises.'

'I think I know what you mean. In the wake of some of recent darker ventures, we at the Wolf Pack have had discussions ... and our conclusions tally with what you seem to be saying.'

'Well, the evidence is there, isn't it ... quite a bit of it that points to something very well hidden and more as time goes by.'

'Yes ... but I'd just like to know ... how much help do you think this Zephyr crowd could be?'

Alex met Damon's eyes, which were an intense, steely blue to his milder, deeper blue.

'I'm barely aware of more than the name ... but from what I understand, this organization has been around for a long time.'

'Long time? Forty, fifty years?'

'No, I think much longer. Maybe add a zero.'

'Oh, that is interesting ... at least from the wealth angle. You can be sure we'll take a look. Thanks for the information.'

'I'm just the messenger in this instance but I think we can all be safe in assuming that things are only going to get worse. I hear the new covid variants in Europe are astonishing ... they seem to be taking over the minds of victims and driving them crazy in various ways. I'm glad that we have border controls.'

'Me too. Yet it's been going on longer that you'd think. Our tech guy's been keeping an eye on these weird psychological strains for a few years and there have been cases here as well. They hit the poor and the seedy worst and we don't see a lot of it in the wealthier enclaves but the range of effects is actually quite staggering.

'Our operatives come into contact with these sorts of people more often than they would like and in many cases, they simply have to call the ambos and have them dragged off ... but not before they get blood samples.'

'Your people have been taking blood samples?" Alex exclaimed. 'That's crazy.'

'Don't worry, our operatives are trained to deal with it and our tech guy is brilliant. I hope you can meet him one day because he's a hoot.'

'One day.'

'Yes, hopefully in better days. You know that if we didn't deal with these people, the RED would deal with them, don't you?'

'The RED?'

'Oh, you haven't heard of them. Sort of independent government trouble shooting organization.'

'Why do they call it RED?'

'Ready extermination division.'

Cara went pale and Alex's features froze in horror and anger.

'There's a government extermination service? For people?'

Damon shook his head.

'I've seen that sort of surprise before,' he said. 'Honestly, I kind of get a kick out of it. It started out as a sort of clean up team, the sort of thing we really needed during the pandemic peaks ... but then it became too difficult and dangerous to deal with these crazed sick people ... so they turned to killing them. Easier to handle.

Then it went from killing sick people to killing anyone they didn't like.'

Cara shot up, angry and shaking.

'No. I know the PM. Kane wouldn't allow that sort of thing!'

'Wouldn't allow? He doesn't know of course. They don't want to know when it comes to the more difficult decisions. Why else do you think they appoint these task force heads ... with so many powers?'

'Not know? I'll give him a taste of my tongue that he won't forget.'

'Do it ... by all means. It might get them to ease up a bit on us. Gone are the old days of our simple Robin Hood operations.'

'I didn't know what you had to deal with,' said Alex quietly. 'In truth, I half imagined a bunch of wealthy, spoiled heroes living out their childhood dreams of playing the vigilante.'

Damon smiled.

'Sometimes what we imagine about others is what we are truly most guilty about in ourselves,' he said a little provocatively. 'In truth, Wolf returned only yesterday from a debacle in the city so violent and unbelievable that one could only believe it was invented if one did not know it to be true.'

'Forgive me my ignorance ... seems your people are putting their lives on the line but in truth we are here and we've promised to do what we can to help ... including Zephyr ... and now that I know what I know about you, I'm wondering what Zephyr does.'

'The situation in Britain is bad from all accounts I've heard. The new wave of the pandemic has taken hold with a vengeance there. Of course, there are quite a few groups trying to get the best from it and doing their best to survive ... but none really seem to have a sense of the mission to rebuild our world ... no, in truth to build a better world. This is why we follow Wolf. He sees it so clearly. When we forget why we're here, he reminds us. I've never met anyone like him. He's our leader and he could sit back safe and do my job but he insists on being out there in the thick of things. Without that courage and that sense of commitment, you have what you see in Britain ... increasing fragmentation.'

'Sounds like a big character,' said Cara.

'Yes,' said Alex, old enough and wise enough not to let jealous thoughts intrude.

Cara glanced at him and was reassured to see a breadth and calmness in his expression. That was her man. That was why she loved him. It was, she noted, surprisingly reassuring.

'Anyway ... back to the practical matters,' said Damon, watching the interplay of their expressions. 'It will be easy to set up fund raisers with you two because as I understand it, you've been targeted a bit already. Police know it and just about everyone knows you're swimming in cash. And by the way, we keep a watch on our donors as well. Wouldn't want any harm coming to them, would we?'

'No.'

'Do you have short wave radio?'

'We have one that will pick up just about anything. Picked it up today. Compuscan portable.'

'Excellent, although portable is debatable.'

Alex laughed.

'I'll get Cara to wear it.'

'She does look pretty fit. I'll give you a master code list for a month and we can send messages about ops to each other. It has twelve different sequence combinations so for each month thereafter, go with the one according to the next firing order number of your vee twelve Jag. That way, we'll know its you.'

Damon handed him a finely printed page with all the combinations of codes.

'Nice and simple.'

'It'll get us through a year and after that we can think of something else if we need to.'

On the way home, Cara and Alex did not talk much. There was a lot to absorb from that meeting and both wanted to get everything as clear as possible in their heads. It was not a game, nor was it a story. It was their lives, so they knew they had to get it right.

Alex set up the radio initially in Laughton's boathouse and switched it on with some anticipation. At first, all he heard was a lot of whining and popping and after a while he heard some strange things being said in English by some very dubious types, firstly concerning killing and later concerning children.

That faded away and he retuned. Only moments later he heard cold somehow inhuman voices talking in a completely unfamiliar language. In truth, it was creepy and before long he switched it off, knowing that the following day would probably be a big one.

Things like that increasingly made him feel angry but he also knew that negative realities would always be there if you looked for them. And they had the potential to eat you alive from the inside.

Chapter 16 — NASA Self Destructs

Stan Howe was a cautious man and he could not understand the attitude his colleagues had towards the thieving couple in Australia. Somehow, they had got the Time Vault files and they were making the most of them but they were interlopers — not even American. Cruel fate would have these opportunists enjoying benefits that someone like him might well have enjoyed. He came from a wealthy family but what it would be to have wealth independent of them!

Not exactly young anymore and looking to find a suitable wife, he felt he could even be able to wring something out of this now. President Ashmore might still be persuaded to bring the CIA in on this with greater force. Yes, Australia was an ally but even allies had to toe the line if they wanted to remain allies.

But if his colleagues maintained their current stance there was little chance of that. He would have to stop them — discredit them. Ashmore was renowned for sticking to his advisers' lines so if he got to him first with the right message, he would be that adviser.

At work on Thursday night, May the tenth, still well after his peers had left, he decided to hack into his workmates' files. Mike Carsen and Joe Miller were the two biggest problems. Their approach to this did not make any sense. Why let them get away with the theft of intellectual property worth god knows how many millions — maybe billions?

A contact in the CIA had given him what he had referred to as 'foolproof' hacking software and now was the time to use it. He inserted the USB drive into Miller's computer first and the password caved in less than five seconds. Miraculous!

After half an hour or so he had nothing from the main files of the computer but then he decided to check out Miller's email account — and there it was. It — or them. There were quite a few emails between Miller and Carsen and Weston, the new junior guy. What was he doing in the loop? The bastards had not confided in him but they had with young Weston!

And the emails were discussing exactly what he wanted to see. Apparently, they had suffered some sort of conscience or doubts about all this because none of them seemed absolutely certain that they were doing the right thing. They had discussed the moral implications of releasing all the data to the Jamiesons as well as a number of possible downsides.

He copied as many emails as he could but did not bother to hack into anyone else's computer, given that he had everything he could possibly need, now.

When Howe got back to his own computer, he began drafting his case against his colleagues and spent a couple of hours over it before saving the material and going home.

In the morning, Howe was a little late and Miller had gotten in early. He started his computer up first thing and immediately knew something was wrong. A little red question mark on the bottom right corner of the screen told him that someone had hacked in.

Miller went straight to Carsen and told him.

'Someone's been into my files,' he said. 'I bet you don't need more than one guess as to who.'

'Howe's a bloody try-hard if ever I saw one. I don't think he liked our position with the Jamiesons ... from the word go.'

'You said he'd be trouble. I bet he used that software the CIA's been handing out.'

Carsen laughed.

'Probably thought he was the only one to get it.'

'You keep an eye on the foyer and I'll take a look at his files. Think of an excuse if you can to keep him out of here this morning.'

'That UFO sighting guy. We'll go visit him ... he's got something new.'

Miller logged in pretty quickly, as Howe had, with the same software. There it was right on the desktop. A letter.

Dear Mr President,

I greatly regret to have to tell that my colleagues at NASA have betrayed our country and are scheming with a foreign couple to release sensitive information relating to recent discoveries on Mars.

One can only conclude that bribes have been made and the priorities of these men are unbecoming their responsible office. Disloyalty to America should be a punishable offence. Certainly, where criminals are acting under the guise of establishment scientists, they should be held to account by whatever means.

My God, thought Miller. This guy was aiming to hang them out to dry completely. Such allegations put to the president could get them locked up for good. Clearly, Howe had never intended discussing any of the pros or cons of their decisions. They were a team and habitually discussed any matters of importance but Howe had typically remained very quiet. Just what was he?

Miller shut down the computer and only a couple of minutes later Howe entered with Carsen at his shoulder.

'Was just telling Howe, here, that we've decided to go and see this fellow with all the UFO photos. Likely they're all fakes but we need to get it out of the way.'

'Sure. Up on the north-west side, isn't he?'

'Yes, Wakefield. We'll take the train and get off at Tenleytown. Fine morning outside.'

'I'm busy,' said Howe stubbornly. I'll sit this one out.'

'Oh no you won't,' said Miller. 'You're the one who first took a call from this guy. It's your gig. We're only coming along to keep you company.'

'I guess what I'm doing can wait.'

'Sure as hell it can. What's so important anyway?'

'Oh, nothing ... just some research into some possible funding sources.'

Miller smiled wryly.

'Thought we had that all covered. Government, right?'

'New programs. Don't care who pays for them.'

'Then you're right, it can wait. Go arrange transport to the station.'

Miller practically chivvied him out the door then took the opportunity to quickly talk to Carsen.

'He's drafted a letter to the President accusing us of criminal activities. Ashmore's a stickler for following advice and sticking to the rules ... or being seen to be. We'll be toast. We've got to think of something.'

Carsen shrugged his shoulders.

'Draft a counter letter detailing this guy's weaknesses and shortcomings. He's lazy, doesn't contribute to group discussion. What about expenses?'

'Yeah, I've had to pull him up on that a few times,' Miller conceded. 'It might work ... but on what excuse do we approach the president about this?'

'You don't. Departmental complaint ... goes on the record ... prompted by laziness and dereliction of duty ... insubordination.'

'Yes, of course but it doesn't stop the fact that we are on shaky ground with the Jamiesons. Fact is, we can't prove they did anything wrong but neither should we be supporting them without the proper grounds.'

'What are the proper grounds?' Carsen asked.

'We're scientists. Our job is to make discoveries but you could also say that it is also our moral duty to make sure those discoveries are disseminated.'

'To the wider community. Yes, and that's exactly what we're doing. The situation was complex. It called for unusual measures. What was I thinking? We're not on shaky ground at all.'

'Not if it's put on show the right way ... quickly. We could also draft plans to publicize our connection ... back the novels as remarkable creative parallels of scientific discovery that we can and do sponsor.'

'In for a penny, in for a pound, huh. I think it'll work. So up front with it all that even the president couldn't think the worst.'

'Excellent. Let's get going ... but take your laptop and start working on that sponsorship deal. I'll do the same in any spare moments to draft this departmental complaint.'

Out on East Street, on which the Mary W Jackson Nasa Headquarters was located, they found a taxi quickly enough and it took them to Judiciary Square Station.

Carsen decided to engage Howe in conversation about the relative merits of communication. It seemed like a good defence to winkle something out of him that could be seen to support their stand on this issue and surprisingly, he responded with vigour.

'Of course, communication is important,' Howe said in response to a proposition that it was vital. 'It's like that fellow Jamieson said, we build our world around words ... but there is a time and a place.'

They got out of the taxi and Carsen sought his eyes.

'Are you saying that the world isn't ready for what we discovered on Mars?'

'I'm saying that we might not be the best judges of whether it is or not.'

'Why not? We're scientists. We discovered it. We should know what's good for our fellow man.'

Howe seemed to squirm as they walked over towards the crossing and fought his eyes away from Carsen's intense gaze.

'We're specialists. It doesn't make us the best judges of this kind of thing. I'm a bio-archaeologist. You're a thrust dynamics expert. Billings is an astrophysicist.'

'But we're all still people, right, and our qualifications make us better qualified than average to judge what's good for our fellow man.'

Howe started to get angry then.

'By the powers of hell, your hubris is dangerous, friend. Have you ever thought what these texts might do to society? You all seem to suck up this idea that we'll be somehow better off for following some alien's ideas about how to live ... but things will change. We have a comfortable status quo now ...'

Howe approached the kerb and turning to meet Carsen's eyes again in an attack reciprocal to what he had felt only moments earlier, stepped off.

Carsen met his eyes but only for a second. As Howe stepped off the kerb there was a shriek of brakes and a bus slammed straight into him with a sickening thud. Howe's eyes were torn away from his.

Chapter 17 — Back in the Bush

Around a week after Howe's death, on Saturday the nineteenth, Alex considered what Damon had told him only the day before. Even now, in the E-type under the midday sun, heading down to the Cove, he could not get the conversation or the ramifications of the issues it had raised out of his mind.

There had been cases of the new covid strain here — quite a few it seemed — but the government had an efficient extermination service. Perhaps it was that alone which had saved Australia from the massive spread of insanity that was afflicting most other nations.

Could PM Kane's moral cowardice have saved the country from a horrific fate? If that really was the case, what did it say about the state of things? The more he thought about it, the more he realized how important it was to have a Wolf Pack or something like it, and how important it was to support it.

Damon had an air of strength held in disciplined reserve. He did not seem like any kind of 'Boys Own' character he had ever encountered. If he was disciplined and careful, Wolf would be as well, especially given that Damon admired him so much.

Cara was following him in the Ineos otherwise he would have said to her: 'Thank god we have a Wolf Pack.' He even imagined her saying: 'Well, we're in the thick of it now, aren't we?'

For a moment he thought about calling her but knew in a second that he should never even make mention the

Wolf Pack while on the phone. No doubt, every agency under the sun already knew about it but they did not, nor should they ever, know that he or Cara had a relationship with them.

When they arrived back into the Rocky Plains area, they were both interested and relieved to find that the start of the Wainui Road was now policed by a couple of young fellows in a farm ute.

Alex stopped and Cara pulled up behind him. One of them was Ben's son Jay.

'Everything okay, mate?'

'All good Alex. Let a couple of tourists through a while ago but everyone knows they're in our locality and they'll keep an eye on them. Older couple with a van.'

'Well, there's trouble for sure!'

They laughed.

'This is m' mate, Rod,' said Jay.

'Good thing you're doing here. Eucumbene Road and Rocky Plains Road covered too?'

'We've even got a team on Happy Jack's. Damn gate wouldn't stop any arseholes.'

'Can't believe we've still got a locked gate on that road since Parks is gone.'

'We control it now,' said Jay. 'I'll give you a key.'

Once they arrived back at the house, late Saturday afternoon, it didn't take long for Cara to raise the same issues that he had been thinking about.

'I never realized before how much we need those guys in the River,' she said. 'I don't think we can do enough for them.'

'I agree ... but we do have to stick to the plan ... let them dictate the times, the places, the amounts taken. They know what they're dealing with and we shouldn't do any more than they ask.'

'Yes, I see what you mean. They must be treading a fine line, what with the RED and all.'

'I'd like to write their story too, when this is all over. What a thing it would make with all the Reign of the Dragon and Rings of Fate stories.'

'Twenty thousand years ago on another world then moving on to Earth. That culture and its disappearance and then us still fighting evil here in the twenty first century. Yes, a vast panorama of time.'

Alex shook his head while pouring a couple of Apple Thief ciders.

'And don't forget that the 'Reign of the Dragon' gives us limited information about Arya even up to a hundred and twenty thousand years ago.'

'Hard to imagine.'

'In a way but really, why do we not have accounts from our forebears of long ago? Books apparently existed a very long time ago. One can only conclude that they've all been destroyed.'

Cara looked at him with realization in her eyes as she unpacked the contents of her car fridge into the kitchen fridge.

'We'll have to make sure that all this remains on the record, like Thor did.'

'Gold leaf books?'

'Maybe. All sorts of things. Buried flash discs and the like. Is there some sort of permanent paper?'

'Archival paper and I've heard Sumi ink is good but they reckon the paper only lasts about three hundred years.'

'Not good enough,' she said.

'Maybe we can invent something.'

'What ... laser etched sheets of stainless steel?'

'Or titanium?'

'It's quite brittle,' Alex told her, taking a sip of the mead he had poured.

'Then maybe titanium coated stainless? It needs to last at least three thousand years in protected conditions. Based on what we've read, there seem to be quite a few three thousand-year cycles.'

'Yes, I hadn't really processed that. My god, it's strange ... to be part of this knowledge ... and to be part of preserving it. You're right, I'll find an engineering firm to get this started.'

'Tomorrow?'

'Tomorrow.'

While Cara got dinner sorted, Alex set up the Compuscan in the large loft behind the main bedroom. It was a well integrated unit and all he had to do to get it running efficiently was to put the primary dish on the roof and plug the main unit into the power. He secured the dish to the main satellite dish with a little rope and duct tape then swapped over the connections, which were the same.

Inside, he plugged in the satellite cable to the Compuscan, which he had set up on a small table. Well before Cara had dinner ready, he had it switched on and was conducting an auto search. Then he went to dinner.

When he returned, it was about nine o'clock and there was still only a bunch of relatively uninteresting stuff.

Strangely, at almost the same time, early on Saturday morning, half a world away, Joe Miller of NASA instructed Perseverance on Mars to do a new search with a variety of new parameters, all of which involved emitting various electromagnetic waves. After trying a few kinds, they came to infrared and when they did, something astonishing happened.

With events as they were in Washington DC, NASA was in turmoil. A scientist had been killed and a number of strange circumstances had been uncovered. Enquiries had been instigated and more were in the wind.

These events had precipitated independent action on the part of some of the senior NASA scientists and part of this action was Joe Miller's initiation of the new search at seven in the morning DC time, before senior leadership had made it in to work.

If the measures had been executed later, things might have panned out differently but as it was, when the signal from Mars began transmitting, Alex Jamieson was at the ready seated before the Compuscan and recording while he listened. NASA had access to measures that might have been able to block the signal but with so few present in the building at that hour, Joe was unable to engage the jammer in time.

The broadcast only lasted thirty seconds or so and by the time he had gotten over his shock and lunged for the right panel, it was all done and dusted. Who might have heard it also, he had no idea but he hoped that no one would have been ready with the sort of equipment needed to analyse and translate the material.

Joe was wrong. Alex felt driven now by need to expose the corrupt and the careless. He was on fire that night and so, on the ball. When the signal came, he had it all in seconds and in the next few minutes made five copies in various forms both on his computers and on the best four USB drives.

Holly, the translator, would be arriving tomorrow but even now he could start the process. He called Cara up into the loft to hear the news and she sat down with eyes wide. When she heard it, she settled in to assist him with the initial translation work, using the same program and matrix employed with the original files.

'There's definitely enough data here for at least five or six books of about the same length as the books in the Dragon series,' said Alex while he was setting up a text file for the translation.

'These are the same characters that were used in the original files,' Cara noted. 'I recognize these in this title. The one in the middle means "of"!'

'And the first one is the ... the rings ...'

'The Rings of Fate ... it has to be.'

'It is. It is! We have it, baby. We have it!'

'Why did it transmit?'

'Someone must have followed my advice and got the rover to emit some UV or infra red ... or something. They did it ... and damn but look at the time. DC is fourteen hours back. It would have been not long after seven in the morning. Someone's taken a big risk and got into work early to initiate the search!'

'Then we still have friends there?' said Cara.

'Maybe, maybe not. There were some weird noises only seconds after the transmission stopped. I think it might have been some sort of jamming but it was switched on just too late.'

'Maybe to cover themselves.'

'Or try to. If they did this without permission they'll still be in trouble.'

'But maybe not get the sack if they tried to jam it.'

'Until they learn that someone did get it,' said Alex. 'Then they might be in for worse than sacking. Wonder if they have ever given it to us like they agreed to.'

Cara shook her head.

'I believe they have need of a Wolf Pack in the USA, as well,' she said.

Holly arrived about ten the following day, Sunday, having stayed in a motel in Canberra. Snow overnight had made it impossible for her small car to get through so they drove down to the Jindabyne Road in the Ineos to pick her up.

Unknown to Alex and Cara, Wolf Ballantyne was also in the Snowies in the company of a young woman from Tasmania he had just rescued from a dangerous situation. He was on a property higher on the range along the Snowy Mountains Highway.

Alex and Cara already had the books translated by the time they went to pick Holly up and knew for sure that it was the first of the lost series, The Rings of Fate. Its title was "Troll Slayers of Midgard" and it told the story of an ancient tribe of men called Archers, who were friendly with a mysterious druid called Godolphin. The story opened with him offering two of them a brief history lesson from times ancient even to them.

The main character, Rafe Bowman, had found a magical item — a ring that Godolphin considered to be one of great power. To Alex and the others at the outset, it seemed very similar to Lord of the Rings, but it quickly became apparent that it was more real time historical and geographically factual.

The world was Midgard, rather than fictional Middle Earth. The Archers were smaller than men but not by a lot — and unlike hobbits, they were capable and fierce enough to defend themselves in a clearly dangerous world.

The Norse gods were known to these people although they were referred to generally by another name — The Avaltriki, which Holly told them meant Always Rulers or Eternal Rulers.

Moving forward, the second chapter led straight into describing the adventurous lives of these people hunting vile creatures called 'orcne', small yet violent and repugnant creatures of unknown origins, as well as trolls, which were much larger and more dangerous.

'From the background in the Dragon series,' said Holly, 'we have to deduce that all this started on Earth about twenty thousand years ago and that the story we're reading now was only about seven thousand years ago ... but this tale is remarkable. It's like Tolkien's work but through a different lense. If it is some sort of genuine history, it will give us a detailed look into times that we have never seen before ... about which we currently know almost nothing.'

'Perhaps it is that,' Alex observed, 'but we'll need to read further to get definitive answers. We don't really know at this point. It does take the form of a series of tales, after all, and might only be myth.'

Holly frowned, apparently disappointed with that assessment.

'Well, the same could be said of the Dragon series,' she replied, 'and why would people go to so much trouble to hide and preserve these stories, if they were not at least to some extent histories?'

'Even if they're not,' said Cara, 'they do have value ... great value in ways that our world currently needs. Were they seers, these people ... and could they have had foreknowledge of our situation?'

Alex shook his head.

'I don't think they would have needed to be seers to understand our likely needs,' he said. 'All it required was to know what it was to be human ... to be a well for the truth ... and to have wisdom. With that, they could have guessed the plight of any human society in the future.'

Cara sighed.

'Oh, of course,' she said, 'the eternal struggle of good against evil ... of truth against deceit and beauty in the face of ugliness?'

'When you put it that way, I hope not ... at least not the eternal side of it. The idea of eternal struggle can become wearying.'

Cara jumped up and flashed a broad grin across her face, standing with her hands on her hips and her feet wide in a stance of apparent readiness.

'You don't mean that,' she said. 'It's all way too exciting to be wearying. You know that we're part of something big and beautiful in this ... something that'll set back the darkness such a long way it might be ten thousand years before it even gets so much as a look-in again.'

Alex laughed and jumped up to join her.

'You're a live one, Cara,' he said, happily. 'One in a million. Yes, we do need to be steady and true ... holding onto the positive like our lives depend on it. We'll damn well give it our best.'

Holly was envious. This couple were famous, beautiful and wealthy. They even had wisdom. Yet one could not resist. You had to go one way or another in the face of it and she chose to go with the light. Something about the way Cara looked at her just then sealed the deal for good and all. She had always loved Cara and Cara had always been good to her.

'Some of us with less to rejoice in might not have that sort of energy,' she said in the end, 'but it doesn't need to stop there. Most people want to be constructive and fair and right thinking but they do need motivation ... and from what I've read so far, I think these books will do that. We need to know that we can stand up, stand together and resist the venom that's manifesting throughout the world.'

'Yes, it's easy to say it's just too hard,' Cara agreed, 'but when we see others rising to the challenge ... or read about others rising to their challenges ...'

'It can change us,' Alex said quietly, finishing her sentence for her.

That night, Cara and Alex slept with Holly on the lounge. Holly nodded off first, then Cara. Alex fed the fire before turning out the lights.

About three in the morning, he woke again into a lucid dream and almost immediately encountered Seria, who seemed more grand and beautiful than he remembered.

'I believe you've recovered some tales of Earth's early history ... or at least humanity's early history. It's vital that you understand the depth and significance of these stories of your kind.'

'Vital? Why?'

'You must understand what you've lost ... for who can easily understand what they've lost in themselves when they no longer know it? If you were sad or lonely or sick and knew not what it was to be content and loved and healthy, wouldn't you think that your existence was just normal ... that it was the way it should be?'

'Probably.'

'So, this awareness is crucial and these tales must be disseminated out to as many of your people as possible. Forget the Wolf Pack and Valhalla and all the money that you can spend on these causes, at least for the time being. All that is of little importance compared to what you are doing. Humanity is a creature that can only be healed from within. Everyone has to heal themselves but these tales will assist them ... will open up the path to hope and to love and to truth.'

'Perhaps we have become a little side-tracked,' Alex responded, 'but we are working on checking through the translation and have no intention of leaving it until all is done and the books are released.'

'That's good to hear ... but there may be more that you will have to do and you must remain free and at large to do so.'

'Very well ... but as you say yourself, the dangers are many and right now, we are virtual prisoners in this remote locality. Our politicians are increasingly suspect, the covid variations are becoming horrifically infectious and diabolical. Violence is growing around the world. We can't ignore that and I hope that you are not.'

'Certainly not,' Seria replied, warm light seeming to flow up and out behind her. 'I know my mission and my plans are coming to fruition. You're right that violence has grown terribly around the world but the Wolf Pack has stepped up its game and they will soon be expanding. In truth, there is one thing left that you can do, with regards to them. Remind them that the time has come to seek out Zephyr. Do it now.'

Alex woke straight away. It was around three AM, Tuesday morning. He wondered if he should call Peter straight away then recalled that Damon had given him the means to contact him directly.

He got up and went upstairs to the large loft and switched on the Cumpuscan. The screen glowed red and he pulled out the bit of paper Damon had given him from drawer underneath. Using the code for this day, Tuesday, the twenty-first of August, he drafted a digital signal and sent it with four repeats over a minute.

'Seek the contact I told you about as soon as possible. Urgent, repeat, urgent.'

Chapter 18 — NASA in Chaos

At NASA headquarters, Washington DC, on Monday the twenty-first, the science division was in turmoil. The Chief Scientist, Alain Masters, had recently suffered the misfortune of being separate from his wife but that was the least of his worries. A tall, gangling balding man with beady blue eyes, he was nervous by disposition and since being appointed head, seemed determined to make his subordinates share that nervous misfortune.

After the loss of Stan Howe, he ordered a thorough investigation, sensing in that incident a range of factors that could be used to needle his colleagues. Then there was the fact that the main spook agencies had been putting pressure on him to sound out his staff. To what end none of them had specified but Masters knew what they meant — the higher matter of subservience to whatever seemed imperative at the time.

Knowing full well that Howe had been unpopular amongst most of his senior staff members, he had got him promoted primarily to keep an eye on them — but now he was dead. While the circumstances indicated only a remote possibility of foul play, he would find evidence if he could and to that end he had called in Carsen today to be grilled on a range of recent events, including the strange, unauthorized activation of Perseverance on Saturday morning.

'You know this is a very important matter,' he said to Mike only moments after he entered. 'Your answers to my questions will have a bearing on your future in this department. We can't have staff being pushed under buses every time there's some disagreement.'

Carsen stiffened.

'I don't like the imputation there, Masters. We're scientists here, not murderers. The only thing that you'll find here is that Howe was a bit of a careless cove ... with his work and it seems also with his life. He stepped out in front of that bus while talking.'

'And it just so happened that you were the one he was talking to, moments before it happened.'

'We're not allowed to talk while walking along sidewalks? It's ridiculous.'

'He must have been distracted to do such a thing.'

'Perhaps he was ... but not by me.'

'I'm told he was drafting a complaint against you and your closest colleagues ... about this matter of the Jamiesons ... to the President!'

'I honestly don't know why he objected to the Jamiesons,' said Carsen. 'They're an interesting couple and very good at what they do. And it's totally possible they did have an independent source for their stories. If so, we have to ask what those sources could have been and face the possibility that we could be dealing with powers beyond our experience. That's where they seem to be tuned in. Come to think of it, I think it's likely Howe was envious of them.'

'I'm not so sure about that or even if Howe was wrong. In retrospect, we gave the Jamiesons too much too easily and if I don't do something about this, just for one thing, Richard will be breathing down my neck.'

'What are you planning to do?' Carsen asked.

'We'd decided to give them these books. Dammit, Mike, why do they deserve them? I think we'll delay forwarding the files to them, at the very least. And that brings up the whole issue of Miller's activating Perseverance without permission or notice.'

'But we know that it was the right thing to do and the right thing to give them the data. These stories should be out there for all the world to read.'

'I've had various people tell me they're a destabilising influence.'

Carsen was fuming inside and despite all his debonair subtlety could barely keep the frustration from showing.

'And this world needs to be kept just the way it is because it's so well run, right?'

'Under some circumstances, the status quo is better.'

'I don't think so ... especially not in this case. Nor do any of our team apart from Richard, perhaps. We ... this world's people, do need change and we need it now. And it's not like these books would create the sort of instability that could lead to immediate destructive revolution.'

'We'll put a hold on them, anyway, until I've had time to think about it some more.'

Richard Bain came to see Masters later that morning, not long before he was due to confront Joe Miller.

'I'm getting phone calls from all sorts of people, mostly pretty damn high up, questioning us about what we will do with these Mars files. This decision you've made doesn't hold water.'

'I've reversed it ... for the time being ... a temporary hold until we can get a clearer idea what this might all lead to.'

'Temporary? That's not good enough.'

Masters growled.

'Dammit Bain, you'll get to state your case. What more could you ask for?'

Later that afternoon, Sally from the admin office came around to give her usual bi-weekly report. Masters always locked the doors and drew the curtains for these reports, given to him as they were in a most unusual manner — the girl lying down doggy style and naked tied down hard to a special frame that doubled in his office as a coat rack.

Sally always came in with that demure smile and that intense crimson lip stick. She would slap down the report onto his desk as if it annoyed the hell out of her and he would stand up and remonstrate her, taking her by the arm.

Sometimes he would simply strip her then push her down and fuck her and other times he would hold her hard against the desk and strip her piece by piece then throw down onto the frame. He would then tie her to it by her wrists and ankles.

Best thing about it was that she would never tell anyone because he had caught her thieving from one of the minor maintenance accounts and because her parents were devout Baptists — and in any case, he reminded himself, she liked it.

On Thursday, the twenty-fourth, things got really out of hand at NASA HQ. Richard Bain came to Masters with a proposition to sue the Jamiesons and try to make them prove where they had got the Dragon series from but Masters knew that it would not wash. They were not US citizens in any case, and there was no way of proving anything either way. But Bain pushed it and started to take Howe's line of there being a conspiracy to defraud the American government.

'The CIA doesn't like it, the President doesn't like and the people won't like it either,' Bain argued. 'If you won't start action against them, there'll be hell to pay.'

'What do you mean?'

'I mean there are elements higher up that remain secret and they control everything. You ought to know that. And they're not happy. My contact in the CIA couldn't look at me. Couldn't meet my eyes. We're in big trouble, Alain. You've got no idea.'

'Us?'

'And then there's the Jamiesons themselves. You don't think they'll get off scot free do you?'

'But they're ... not the enemy.'

'Maybe they are and maybe they aren't but up top doesn't like them. Of that you can be sure.'

'But that would be criminal ... if what you're suggesting ...'

'Nobody ever said these elements weren't criminal, least of all me ... but face it, man, they're still the ones in control.'

Later that morning, news came that young Weston was dead. A car crash on his way to work but word was there had been a mystery car involved — a black SUV. Masters knew that things had become dangerous and others were twigging too.

Sally delivered her bi-weekly report that day but Masters' mind was elsewhere for the first time in the year and a half she had been giving it to him.

This time he finished quickly and got up to pull the belt out from his pants. In moments, he pushed her down again as she tried to get up and whipped her, five times, lashing her backside brutally. Somehow it relieved him of all the tension that had been building but in this moment of craziness seemed to have no idea what trouble it could bring him.

She began to cry.

'There's no need for that sort of thing,' she said tearily as she got up and dressed, covering her trim figure for the first time in a way that suggested shame.

'I thought you'd like it.'

'You didn't ask ... and no, I didn't.'

She was thinking now of the new guy down in maintenance. He seemed very protective of her and she knew by now that she had had enough of this.

In truth, the maintenance guy was more exciting. There was that air of something about him and she had encouraged him recently with some success. Since then, he had kept a closer eye on her.

Later in the week, the next time she was due to give her report, he followed her to Masters' office and listened at the door. When he heard strange noises, he forced his way in and caught them in the act.

In a jealous rage, he struck Masters with a wrench and whisked Sally away. When Carsen found Masters, he was near death and by the time the medics got him to the hospital, he was gone. Carsen and Aden James had gone with him in the ambulance.

Neither returned to work that day and when they tried to the next, the whole place was shut down. All they could get out of the police guarding the place was that there had been people murdered.

That evening, the news was out and they were looking for a maintenance worker who was alleged to have killed thirty-five staff, both scientific and administrative, in a strange bloodthirsty rampage. Sally was also missing.

Carsen could not believe it. Masters was dead. Bain was dead. Miller was dead along with many others. Howe was dead. Weston had been killed in that crash not long ago. Many others too, and now young Sally was missing.

Every waking moment he was wondering what was happening and how long it would be before something happened to him. Why? What the hell could have caused all this? The more he thought about it, the less any of these things made any sense.

News of the horrific events at NASA HQ went out to the world and reached the Jamiesons on the afternoon of Friday, May the twenty-fifth. Not long after that, Damon appeared at the back door of the Cove house and Alex was surprised because he had heard no vehicle approach.

'How did you get here?'

'Don't ask. You'd probably fall over backwards but suffice it to say that your little early morning message to me resulted in a significant outcome and I wanted to come and thank you personally.'

Alex invited him in. It was still very cold outside with some snow hanging around.

'That big?' he said when they were comfortably by the fire.

Cara came and sat down near them. Holly was still at work upstairs.

'It's amazing how this is all coming together,' Damon continued, We've been working on remote viewing and it turns out that at the same time Wolf was perfecting it used it to get in touch someone important ... and I guarantee that you'll never guess who.'

Alex shook his head, well able to guess but not able to actually believe what he was thinking.

'Thor ... from Arya,' he said, almost under his breath.

'How did you know?'

'Just seemed to make sense. After all, you were talking about remote viewing.'

'Well, there's remote viewing and there's ... I don't know what you'd call something that remote. In any case, it all fell into place at around the same time as we got information that led to connecting us with an organization called Valhalla.'

Alex sat up straight.

'Wolf has really talked to Thor?'

'Yes, and we have talked to Valhalla!'

'Valhalla?'

'The real name of Zephyr ... that organization you put us onto. One day I'd like to know how.'

'I believe I can tell you that now. This woman claims to be of an ancient alien race from a people or a planet called Alden. We met her when we took a walk along a beach and over some hills along the coast, where we found her cottage.'

'An alien?'

'A benevolent alien when apparently there are some pretty malevolent ones out there too.'

'Could she just be a crazy?'

Alex shook his head.

'Well, you said Wolf talked to Thor, didn't you? No, when she needs to tell me something, she comes to me in my dreams and I wake up straight away to do whatever needs to be done ... like sending you that radio message. Cara knows her too. She spent a week with us reading all that stuff about Thor before we published.'

Damon looked surprised.

'She didn't know about Thor already?'

'Oh, she knew about him but didn't have all the details of the Aryan histories.'

'Which we all have now, thanks to you. I don't think there's much doubt that they're at least semi historical concerning a particularly significant period in this Aryan culture. And however long ago that was, it seems he's still alive.'

Alex met Damon's impassive eyes closely and decided to take a risk.

'We're working on the lost series now. The Rings of Fate. We received some important data and now it's all coming together. Doesn't seem to have any information in it critical to your operations but Seria says that it's vital for the cultural rebuild this world needs.'

'Seria? The alien woman?'

'Yes.'

'It's so intertwined ... these events.'

'And a long time in the making it would seem,' Alex observed. 'Would you like to see the first chapter of the new series?'

Damon shook his head.

'I'll wait for the formal release. I understand Seria's view on the matter. It will be important but for the time being, we've got too much on our plates to risk letting our focus drift. We have a sort of standoff with the authorities and no idea how long it will last.'

'Of course,' Alex replied.

'Suffice it to say, your information came at a very critical time for us. We also got information on Yagov's whereabouts and sanctioned him so we don't know if there will be retribution or not ... but even if there is, we'll be safer now, thanks to Valhalla.'

Alex knew now how big a part he had played and allowed himself to look pleased.

'Valhalla, huh? Home of Thor and Odin. I wonder how much they've got to do with it.'

'Don't know ... but they're big.'

Alex stood.

They're that big?' he asked. 'Think it could be risky associating with an organization so powerful?'

Damon got up as well.

'Their power is in money and tech. They're mainly academics and scientists with a lot of financial backing and very secure premises. Ideal marriage partner for the Wolf Pack as it turns out.'

'I thought that the Wolf Pack was already married to the Little River.'

Damon grinned.

'Plural marriage, my friend. It has many advantages.'

Just then Holly came down the stairs with laptop in hand.

'Oh, hello,' she said, 'I didn't mean to interrupt but I have to ask you something, Alex.'

Alex grinned briefly at Damon, wide eyed as he was in appreciation of the apparently serendipitous timing of his last comment.

'This is Holly, Damon. Holly's helping us with the translation.'

He nodded to her.

'Oh, so the whole dream thing *was* a lie?'

'With respect to how we got the material, of course. Proving it's another thing, though, so we play the cards as we can.'

'You've done well.'

'So, what is it, Holly?'

'I'm finished with chapter five. It's background with this druid telling Rafe about the history and significance of the High Ring, as they call it ... but it all seems too much like Lord of the Rings. I'm worried that it won't work ... that people will criticize ...'

'You're wondering if it should be released at all.'

'If it's going to cause so much trouble,' she said.

'Well, I think you'll find the story changes pretty significantly as you get into it. Fact is, it is what it is and we can only press on and see how it turns out. And the people are not the same really, are they?'

'No, there are no hobbits and the wizards are druids and they revere the Norse gods. There's no Bilbo and none of that back story about stealing treasure from a dragon's lair.'

'And many things change in the story along the way. It would be too much of a coincidence if everything was the same, wouldn't it?'

'True ... okay, back to work.'

She left and Damon's eyes followed her, dwelling on the spot where she was last visible.

'Oh well,' he said after she was gone. 'I've plenty to do back at the ranch. My place has become the open heart of the Wolf Pack now, since we had all that air combat a couple of days ago.'

Alex regarded him quizzically.

'Air combat?'

'Yes, we had Stingers and Sidewinders and the like streaking through the air over our heads and fighters getting blown to bits within sight of us.'

'So, what saved you?'

'Valhalla. It has some amazing secrets up its sleeve, I can tell you.'

'Dibs on the story when it's all over?' said Alex.

'If I don't write it myself.'

He got up.

'Don't follow me when you go. You'll see it all soon enough but for now, you don't want to know.'

Standing, Alex shook the outstretched hand and nodded with easy understanding.

'You can make your own way out then. Thanks for the update and the appreciation. I really didn't have any idea what I'd be getting into when all this started.'

'Who did?'

'Do you think we'll be alright, here?'

'Don't worry, we're keeping our eyes on you. What you did back there has literally saved our bacon and we won't forget it.'

'Good to know.'

When Damon was gone, Cara went over to Alex and hugged him.

'Can they protect us?' she asked.

'I think so. Something big has just happened to do with that Zephyr crowd. Valhalla, huh?'

'Yeah,' she agreed. 'We've got the stories from long, long ago. Wolf gets a visit or some sort of meeting with Thor by remote viewing and The Wolf Pack gets saved by Valhalla. Are we living some sort of dream?'

'Or nightmare. We're in more danger than I think you realize. These guys have said they're going to protect us but the fact is, we're in the same camp now and it's always more difficult to protect the non-combatants. I've seen things that prove it over and over again in theatres of war.'

Chapter 19 — Deep State Threat

That evening, Cara, Alex and Holly sat around the TV upstairs and saw the whole horrific attack on NASA HQ along with some of the lurid background relating to Sally and her escapades on the Friday night news. The girl was still missing and no one had any reason to think other than that she was captive or dead.

'Do you think that we had anything to do with that?' Cara asked.

'Indirectly, perhaps,' Alex replied with reserve, 'but I kind of predicted it. Sounds like a real mess. They must have been under a great deal of stress.'

'It seems like some of them were pretty irresponsible as well.'

'Doubtless. If there's more like them in positions of responsibility in the states, we might be better off at your father's for the time being. I mean, there are people over there that really don't like us.'

'I was thinking the same thing. Our friends around here are well meaning but could they take on rogue agents from any number of organizations? There are no fences here, no walls, gates or security.'

'I'm guessing it won't take more than a day or two for them to recover from this and start looking for scapegoats ... or just someone to punch.'

'Tomorrow?'

'No, I think, the day after. Don't ask me why but that's what I think.'

Cara smiled.

'I can just see all those strategic wheels turning inside your head.'

'Strategy is a man's best friend, Cara. Besides, the six new books are nearly all knocked into shape now. Another day will do it, I think. Then we can deliver them more or less as soon as we get up to Sydney.'

'You don't think they'll need more editing?'

'Do you?'

'No. They're good. Who wrote these ones I'm not sure but it doesn't exactly seem like the same writer.'

'Or maybe he was just much older when he wrote them.'

'Several thousand years older, maybe.'

Four days later, on the twenty-ninth of May, they had only recently delivered the manuscripts, in company with Holly, when they were outside relaxing on the porch in the afternoon sun, looking out towards the pretty timber boathouse and the jetty, when there was a loud roar from the other side of the house. The ground shook and smoke billowed up over the roof.

Alex jumped up and ran back through the hall, closely followed by Laughton, Cara, Genie and Holly. After a moment of hesitation, he opened the front door and there was his precious E type, burning in the driveway.

'What the hell?'

He was fuming.

'Damn, that's going to make a mess,' said Laughton coolly.

'It's made a mess of my car.'

Carter and two of his men were out there in moments, fighting the fire with some large extinguishers. The fire had not enveloped the whole car and they started to get it under control so Carter came back to speak with his boss.

'That was definitely an explosion, Grant. Not a really big one but not simply a wiring fault or anything of that nature.'

'I know the old girl originally had wiring courtesy of the Prince of Darkness, being English and of that era,' said Alex, 'but it had all been redesigned and replaced not long ago.'

'No, there was some sort of small bomb in it,' said Carter. 'I know because I was watching from upstairs and saw it happen.'

'How long had you been watching the drive?'

'Since you got back. No one came in. No one went out.'

'Then how could they have planted it?' Laughton asked.

'Must have been while you were in town. Did you have anyone stay with the car when you were at the publishers?'

'No.'

Cara and Alex and Holly all exchanged glances, horrified.

'Then why didn't it go off when I started it in the publisher's carpark?'

'Must have been a timed fuse. There wouldn't have been time to wire it into the starter circuit and it would be really hard to access anything like that in such a low car.'

'Yes, the bonnet catch is tricky too.'

Carter met Alex's eyes.

'Maybe they thought you would head straight back to the Cove,' he said. 'You'd have been more than half way there by now.'

'Yes, on a windy, difficult stretch of road, maybe. In these times, they might even have gotten away with killing us without any real investigation.'

'If it had happened at speed on a winding road, that would have been it.'

Police and the fire brigade turned up only minutes later and it took a few hours of talking to get everything settled. Their opinion was the same and the firemen confirmed the use of a small explosive device attached underneath the car.

Dinner was a sombre affair. No one liked to face the idea that someone would want to kill them and even normally spirited Cara was downcast.

On the following day, Alex wanted to fill the deficit and started looking for a replacement car. The Jag was not a complete wreck but would need several months of restoration from the bare chassis up so he took the opportunity to go out and trial something more modern — something that would be designed to resist attack in various ways.

Someone kept an eye on the cars and the walls all the time from then on but four days later again, there was another bomb attack, this time outside the compound in the cul-de-sac. A small electrician's van blew up but the explosion was much larger this time, destroying several vehicles parked nearby.

'I'm calling the PM,' said Laughton only minutes after the house was shaken by the blast and several windows broken. 'This has got to stop. Once is bad enough but clearly these bastards won't stop at that. They have to give us police protection.'

Prime Minister Kane took the call.

'Hello Grant,' he said. 'I'm sorry to hear about all this nonsense. I've got military intelligence on the job along with the Federal Police and a promise from the Premier to get the state bobbies into gear. If I can do anything, I'll do this.'

'We're old friends Tony. A lot of things are falling apart but if we can't count on our childhood friends ...'

'You can. You can. If there's any more trouble there I'll come and see to it personally. Heads will roll.'

'I know the kids have stepped into a minefield with this, Tone, but their intentions are good. We need more people like them, not less.'

'You're totally right ... listen there's a call on the priority phone. Just wait a minute.'

Grant waited and all eyes were on him. He was not accustomed to having the PM put him on hold. They had played together as children and gone through primary and high school as the best of friends. They had also shared each others trials and heartbreaks through college. In truth, they were like family.

Just a few minutes later, Anthony Kane was back on the line.

'Good news, sport. Our people have found the perps. Lucky break. One of them dropped a box with bomb parts on the sidewalk while trying to chuck it into a dumpster ... in full view of an off-duty sergeant. New South Wales Police, yes. Got a bullet in the leg for his trouble but he stunned the bastard.'

'Okay, is he?'

'Yeah, sure, one of the tough ones. The other perp tried to run for it but he took a bullet in the backside. Funny thing was ... they were both conscious for a minute then once they were in cuffs, they just turned up their toes and died.'

'Died? Only one was hit with a bullet, right?'

'Not a lethal injury by all accounts. Very strange. S'pose they could have been the same ones that targeted Alex's E type, huh?'

'Probably. Hope so anyway. Maybe that'll see an end to it.'

'I'm still giving you protection. Play it safe, eh mate?'

'I won't argue with that.'

'I'm told the detail will be there in minutes. Let me know if there's any trouble.'

Alex met Laughton's eye as he got off the phone and he looked positively fierce.

'He's doing his best,' said Laughton, 'and his best is pretty good ... for the moment. They've found the guys who planted the bomb, at least the last one, but apparently they just died before they could be questioned or identified in any way.'

'Died?'

'Not from wounds but something else. Bloody strange I can tell you. Tone said there would be a detail around within minutes. I'll go and meet them.'

'I'd hoped we'd be safer up here than at the Cove,' Alex told Cara when he was gone.

'We are,' she responded. 'I know it was kind of a close call with the Jag but this last bomb seems like an act of desperation ... bravado ... something like that. They knew they couldn't get in to kill us but they went ahead with a strategy that ultimately got them caught ... and dead.'

'Yeah, weird that.'

'All sorts of people are supposed to be protecting us,' said Cara, 'but what it looks like is the bombers were found and apprehended just by pure luck.'

Alex shook his head.

'And a little bravery. Maybe chivalry isn't totally dead yet.'

'Difficult work, that.'

'Damn difficult. Don't think I'd like a bullet in the leg.'

'Anything we can do for him?'

'We'll visit him if we can, eh?'

'Of course.'

It was only the next day when they arranged to go and visit Sergeant Ericson. The nurses showed them through and made the introductions.

'Wanted to come and thank you personally,' said Alex as they approached. 'How are you doing?'

'It's done a bit of damage,' Ericson said gruffly, 'so they reckon I'll be in here for a week. You seem to have put your foot in a bloody hornet's nest, man.'

'We have that ... and there's a lot more to it, sergeant, than meets the eye.'

'Ain't there always. Just walking down to the greengrocers.'

'Well, things are changing and now you're a part of it. Are they looking after you well?'

'Sure, but I'm worried about my wife and daughters, now. Can't keep an eye on them and you know, dammit one thing always seems to lead to another.'

'Would you like security to keep an eye on them?'

'Yes. Too bloody right I would.'

'Done. I'll talk to Laughton's man Carter as soon as we get home and see who he thinks would be best.'

They talked for about half an hour and Alex took a liking to the man. Like most police, he had a certain reserve born of tough experience but he was not a plod and had his eyes open.

They exchanged numbers.

Alex made a point of calling Carter as soon as they left the hospital and Carter promised to call Ericson with a suggestion within the hour.

They were using the Ineos and Cara was driving. A couple of minutes into the drive back to the Bay, Alex suddenly felt drowsy and closed his eyes but instead of falling asleep, a clear vision of Seria appeared before him. She smiled at him reassuringly.

'That was good,' she said. *'Ericson's a good man and he deserves to know that he's supported.'*

'Is there anything you don't know, Seria?' Alex asked.

'Many things,' she replied. *'You wonder at my knowing things that you know but the fact is we do have a psychic link.'*

'Oh, so that's how it is. Well, what's on your mind?'

'Mainly what's on yours ... how to keep you safe. You'll need to get a new car and I know you've been thinking about it ... but you need to get on with it. Get one of the new Koenigsegg Agera Tornados. They're very fast and have a super strong shell. One of our agents works at the Sydney dealership. Go there now.'

'Nice. Just what I wanted.'

'We've got a detour,' Alex told Cara. 'Carrington Motors in the city.'

She nodded and he set the GPS.

Half an hour later they were standing at the front of one of the most spectacular shops in Sydney — a place that only sold cars worth a million dollars and up. It was dazzling.

Bentleys, Maybachs, Lamborghinis, Ferraris, Bugattis, McLarens and Koenigseggs. Many more marques graced the showroom floors but Alex had always fancied a Koenisgsegg Agera and the latest hybrid Agera Tornado was there in the most beautiful deep electric blue he could imagine.

'Is that what you want?' Cara asked.

'Sure is.'

'Not a bit like the Jag.'

'A lot quicker, a lot stronger and a lot safer. Just what we need right now.'

'How many horses?'

'Not too far off two thousand in competition mode.'

'My god, wouldn't it take off?'

'Hopefully not.'

'How much did the Jag have?'

'Around two seventy out of the factory but mine had been modernised and put out near five hundred.'

'Even that's over the top.'

'Maybe, for that car with its basic design and technology ... but with this, you won't notice it so much. If you do anything stupid it'll take over and let you down easy.'

'Anything?'

'Almost anything. It can see the corners and calculate the maximum approach speed. It won't lose traction and it reduces horsepower to about three hundred in any sort of traffic. Honestly, it's one of the safest cars around.'

A salesman approached with the sort of superior smile that only a high-priced car salesman can have but then he recognized them both. Few now had not seen their faces somewhere or other but it almost looked like he had been on the lookout for them.

'My word,' he said, 'what a very great pleasure it is to meet you both. The powerful "it" couple desire a powerful car?'

'The "it" man desires a powerful car,' said Cara with an equally complex smile. 'I drive an Ineos.'

'Don't let her fool you. She also has an Aston Alto only a couple of years old.'

'I'm Manfred Markland,' said the salesman. 'Perhaps not quite the power in the Aston as is hidden under the bonnet of what your husband has locked eyes onto, Mrs Jamieson?'

'I don't think so. It's no slouch but engines seem to get pretty ridiculous in cars now.'

'In luxury cars, madam.'

Cara grinned wickedly.

'Oh ... darling, he called me madam! I don't think anyone has ever called me that before. You will have to buy.'

'Didn't know you fancied it.'

'Neither did I.'

'In any case, I'm pretty much set on it, anyway. How much for the blue beauty, Manfred?'

'It's optioned to the hilt, Mr Jamieson.'

'Call me Alex.'

'Of course, thank you. Just a shade under a million but everything's warranted for ten years. You can't kill these things and the insurance is surprisingly cheap.'

'That's like ten mill old money,' said Cara.

'Yes,' Manfred replied, 'but there really is nothing like these.'

'Yes, I've read about these new Ageras. I've always liked them but the features of this latest generation totally pushed me over the line.'

'You like the colour?'

'Perfect.'

'The interior?'

The leather was in interesting fusion of grey green and a delicious pink and it looked utterly luxurious.

'From here. I'll try it for size, shall I?'

'Absolutely.'

Alex and Cara sat inside and Cara was won over instantly.

'I think I want one too,' she said under her breath.

'We can see to that,' said Manfred, 'but perhaps there will be a few months wait.'

'Why is this one available?'

'It was the manager's choice but things are slow and he decided to make it available ... only yesterday. It's only been here a few days.'

'Then you'll take nine hundred kay?'

Manfred laughed and somehow the laugh told them that he knew they were pulling his leg.

'You creative types have such senses of humour. I tell you what, we'll throw in a crate of Moe.'

Alex grinned.

'See, darling, what a little silly banter can get you. We'll be out of it for weeks.'

Manfred leaned in a little towards Cara so that he could lower his voice and still have Alex hear him.

'That would perhaps not be wise given the state of things,' he said. 'I have been asked to deliver a message to you from one of our favoured customers.'

'Who?' Cara asked.

'The prowling creature would rather remain incognito, Mrs Jamieson.'

'You can call me Cara.'

That was delivered with another complex smile.

'Thank you, Cara. It is simply that he has some free time ... rather unusual I would say ... and would like to speak with you.'

Alex moved across a little so he was almost leaning on Cara.

'You can tell him that he is welcome to come and see us anytime.'

'Very good, Alex. I will relay the message. Now to business.'

'Yes.'

'We will have to secure some details before giving you a test drive ... and given the relative complexities ...'

'I'll sit in the back,' said Cara.

'Thank you. You will enjoy this vehicle ... both of you ... and it will serve you well. When our friend also chooses such a thing, you know that it will run.'

'I believe it will.'

'I have also been tasked to tell you that your recent trials have set the team on high alert. Our friend has very little trust in the police and has been exerting a good deal of pressure on them. I can assure you there is a presence beyond the police presence that is both ongoing and unyielding.'

'I'm very glad to hear it,' Alex said. 'We're doing our bit and running the gauntlet as a result.'

'Our friend hears you. I believe he runs the gauntlet as well and knows well how uncomfortable it feels. Yet he is very grateful as well, now things are moving forward.'

'Then the gratitude is mutual. Please tell him that.'

'You might see him before I do ... but at the earliest possibility, I shall tell him you said so.'

Chapter 20 — Friends in High Places

Alex and Cara had enjoyed their new Agera for less than a day before their pleasure was dimmed somewhat by the constant presence of crowds outside the Laughton walls — crowds that very soon turned into rioting ones.

Police responded to these disturbances with perhaps over-zealous impatience and before long, certain individuals had begun to steer things within that crowd towards greater chaos.

Key players from the Wolf Pack were there amongst the crowd, unidentified and unobtrusive, and managed through their subtlety and expertise to hold back the rioting from getting completely out of control.

The sixth of the sixth, forty-six, might in some eyes have seemed deserving of being an auspicious date but in truth, others would have said that it represented the innate conflict between care and pragmatism.

Alex knew that there were those outside who cared about what happened to him and his family but he was never completely sure throughout that day and many others whether pragmatic concerns would get in the way of their being looked after.

A least half a dozen times, he went and checked out the road outside from the highest window in the house and also made several trips out to the boathouse to check over the jetboat, start it and ensure it was fully fuelled and ready to go.

A little after midday, he took it over to Doyle's at Watsons Bay with Carter and one of his guys to buy a seafood lunch for everyone. He went in with Carter and nobody recognized him, wearing a large coat with a hood and sunglasses as he was. It was strangely relaxing to be out completely incognito and Carter could see that it was, grinning at him conspiratorially when they came out loaded with two large bags of seafood.

Just after lunch, Grant took a call from the PM, who asked them in passing to come over to Kirribilli House for lunch on the day after tomorrow. There was a lot to discuss in the current situation and he said he felt for them cooped up as they were.

Friday came and they were indeed still cooped up by the recurring crowds, mostly peaceful but occasionally noisy and obnoxious.

Carter drove the party of five over in the jetboat and he and one of his men remained with it while the family were inside.

Security agents escorted them up the hill and into the grand old building, where Tony Kane was in the vestibule waiting for them.

'Grant, it's been too long. Cara, my dear and Alex I've heard a lot about you. Sorry I couldn't make it to the wedding. Overseas at the time actually.'

'No problems Mr Prime Minister, we've brought Holly Robinson as well, who has been helping us with the books.'

'Bah ... call me Tony, son. Nice to meet you Holly. Must have been fascinating working on the books.'

'Have you read any of the first series, Tony?' Holly asked. 'The Reign of the Dragon series.'

'Of course, young lady, of course. A good deal for us leaders to learn from them, I have to say. I've nearly finished the fourth book but I was told to skip ahead to 'Peace of the Hammer' for the leadership insights it offers ... and I read that after the first.'

'Sure has some things to say, doesn't he?' said Cara.

'*He* does?'

'We assume that Thor wrote them. There are a good many unique insights in these writings that could scarcely have been provided except by him or at least someone very close to him.'

'Well, just because the scripts came from unusual sources ... whether dreams or data from a lava tube on Mars, doesn't necessarily mean all this is true.'

Alex shook his head.

'Ah, Tony, let's not be so ready to fall into the slathering jaws of fallacy. Whether or not these stories are factual does not bear on whether or not they are true. They're true because the insights in them make the best of sense in a clear and logical fashion.'

The PM nodded appreciatively.

'Indeed, they do,' he admitted. 'If only everything had a logical answer. Please, come into the dining room. We've got something special prepared for you all. Take a look around afterwards by all means but I never know when I'll be dragged off somewhere at short notice so let's just enjoy lunch while we can.'

Kane showed them through into the dining room and everything was set formally with excellent soft lighting and low, gentle music — a Chopin piano selection in fact.

They took seat at the upper end of the table with Grant and Kara next to the PM. He was a rather short individual but had an engaging face with alert clear rather pale blue eyes.

'I'm not complaining,' Kane said after they were seated and served with the entrees, 'but you've probably no idea the amount of trouble these books have caused me. Scarcely an hour goes by each day without some American or other calling me with an opinion. Some of them none too pleasant, I can tell you.'

'That's because of their meaning, Tony,' Grant observed. 'You know that you and I discussed this sort of thing as teenagers, numerous times as I recall ... and here we have someone who has genuine answers.'

'Bloody strange, really. Never thought I'd see the day something like this happened. Anyway, we're doing all we can to shield you from the worst of their ire. Don't know what else I can do, really.'

Cara fixed him with a steely gaze.

'Don't you? I can tell you. Make sure our books are set reading in all the high schools and universities. Have a team of your best bureaucrats sift them for practical applications and make sure they're adopted. Call someone at the ABC to tell them to give up their incessant criticism of them.'

'Interesting thought.'

'More than interesting, Tony. This is a once in a lifetime opportunity.'

'To do what?'

'To institute real change. I hope you read Peace of the Hammer again after you've read all the others. It will all become clearer to you then.'

'Once in a lifetime?' said Alex. 'More like this is a once in a thousand lifetimes opportunity ... and who would not want to get things right if there was the remotest possibility of doing so?'

'Yes, of course, of course. We all must do our best. You, know, Alex, your father-in-law was not telling tall stories when he said we talked about improving things, even way back then. We felt the need deeply and worked hard to achieve what we could. But there are always practical limitations ... and everything is more complex than one ever thinks at that age.'

'Complex?'

'Well, yes. It's always about people. So many different people want so many different things. You can't please everybody.'

Alex grinned amiably.

'And that's exactly why we need to make sure we do please some.'

'Even that can be difficult.'

'Yes,' said Grant. 'I've seen it too. Even little things can present huge obstacles. That's why we operate on principles. They give us strength ... the strength to overcome criticisms and niggling details. We drive things through on the strength of principle because we know they are fundamentally right.'

Kane looked grim and a little downcast.

'I know you're right and I must say that I don't hear this sort of thing nearly often enough. You know they say that it's lonely at the top ... well it is. It's hard just to find time to talk to people in a natural way like we are now. It kind of stiffens one. One learns to resent it.'

Cara met his eyes as they lifted again, downcast as they had been.

'Then you must make time,' she said, lightly. 'You must see to that.'

'Yes, I should and I will. It's a grave mistake you know ... we come into jobs like this thinking we have all the answers ... but we don't. We only get the answers we need if we listen.'

'And act.'

Kane looked at her critically.

'Yes, if it's warranted.'

'Well, in our case it is. The way it seems to me, Mr Prime Minister, is that this country is falling apart at the seams.'

'No, we're keeping order very well. Look at the riots outside your own home. Controlled, not stopped but the danger is kept to a minimum.'

'With, as the grapevine tells me, some outside assistance,' Alex remarked. 'The fact is, we all need to look beyond the obvious in the way we do things, now. Thor's conclusions in Peace of the Hammer were that leadership was much more than simply gaining and keeping power ... more than just maintaining order and the show of justice. He always seemed to see the opportunity to make a significant and valuable change and yes, to create a better world.'

'That's a big ask for someone like me. I'm really just a very ordinary bloke.'

Holly laughed and Cara joined her, both with glasses of champagne in their hands.

'Really, Tony? Then surely the onus is on you to find a true man of character to take your place. Thor chose Verilisim on Niflheim to promote as a leader because he had character and integrity. He was also willing to learn from an old enemy because the Keisari had been so successful in defeating them. Now there's integrity! Learn from your former enemy.'

At this point, Tony Kane was feeling somewhat besieged and wondered at his own folly of having invited these people to lunch but in truth he was still, after a little time, able to see himself with degree of objectivity and could take being a little humbled by them.

They were a tall order — famous, wealthy, intelligent and beautiful — in Cara and Holly's case. Even Genie was still quite a picture.

'I take your point,' he said at last with a big sigh. 'I don't really measure up but the fact is I really don't know anyone willing to do the job who does either. You have to remember that Thor was operating under a sort of feudal monarchy system and he was the product of hundreds of generations of breeding. We just don't have that sort of human resource, here ... perhaps not anywhere on this planet.'

'Well, sir,' said Cara, 'that is why these books are so very important to us all. We live in a world festering in corruption where so many aspects of life literally are falling apart at the seams ... and just in the nick of time, there are all the answers we need, right before us! I don't believe the inspiration in them that we have facilitated will fall on deaf ears but if you stand on the side of the angels, why would you not do your utmost to make sure that voice is heard?'

'Do you think that voice ... those ideas, could work here ... that such a system as Thor administered could work here, in this time?'

'Yes. I believe it could.'

'That might be the case but if it is, it would not be up to one such as me to make it happen. I think you know that. I'm the band-aid ... not the cure.'

Alex looked at greying old Tony with something akin to admiration in his eyes.

'You can see yourself then, with a degree of clarity,' he observed. 'Yet you still allow organizations like the RED to run wild in our country.'

'The RED might not seem necessary at the moment but it has been and it will be again. You shouldn't really know about it, Alex, but old school journo as you are, I shouldn't be too surprised.'

Alex held his gaze fast.

'But from what I hear, you either don't have close enough control over it or you've appointed the wrong guy to control it. Its mission, as I understand it, was to dispose of biological threats to the community ... but it appears to have become political and a deadly tool for exerting ideological control.'

Kane looked grim.

'You may be right,' he said quietly. 'It's not something I ever wanted much part of ... and to be honest I was probably being squeamish. I suspect now, however, that it is not something I could easily gain control over again. It was always the dark side and it has only gotten darker. There are those who have set themselves up to do battle with these sorts of things and they are better equipped to deal with them than I.'

Grant and Alex both realized what he was saying at the same time and were amazed.

'You are a friend, indeed,' said Grant.

'Of course I am. Understand me folks, there are forces at work in this world that cannot easily be gainsaid let alone controlled or defeated. Yet, natural enemies will generate their own predators and we must let the foxes run free to eat the rats.'

'Perhaps after all you do have your own kind of wisdom,' Alex remarked.

Kane stood and raised his glass.

'Then we have a truce, my friends, and let us raise our glasses to drink to the foxes. May they run free and dine well!'

'Hear, hear to freedom!' said all those around the table in unison.

Everyone sat down again but Alex had not done yet and looked hard at Kane.

'I understand that you may not have given yourself over to the darkness as we suspected but at the moment it reigns both within and without and I would ask you one favour still if you could.'

'What, lad, what?'

'You are technically our leader and have considerable influence. We seem to be facing daily threats as a family and it's entirely possible that we will not see through to the new year alive. I appeal to you to use whatever you can to influence the Americans. Hold up a trade deal, expel an ambassador, put an American CEO in Australia up on charges ... whatever it takes to get them to call off their dogs from our gate!'

Kane nodded.

'Yes, I understand how you must be feeling, which was in fact why I asked you here today. I can't see any merit in our literary champions being made martyrs ... so I will do what I can. The dark agents of the American deep state can go fuck themselves. I'll see if we can't get some of those American angels in to deal with them, well out of our way, instead.'

Again, he stood and raised his glass and the others followed suit, confident that that they had bought a little time in the path of this grim sequence.

Chapter 21 — The President Overthrown

No one in the Laughton and Jamieson extended family quite realized how far the issue had gone by early in July and how seriously everyday people everywhere were taking it. It took Carter to point out to them just how huge it had all become on Truth and X.

Whether the Australian PM's throwing out the US ambassador had much to do with it or not no one really knew but not long after that, protests and rallies had become so huge in the US that they were like armies ... or civilian militia.

People were tired of black ops and the dark face of the US deep state establishment. They had been heartened, along with people in many other nations around the world, by the stories of Thor and the Aryan people — another and greater world of humans however long ago and far away it was.

When it came out that the celebrated authors of these books were being harried, threatened and targeted for assassination, a great many people became angry — very angry with their government.

President Ashmore had personally contacted PM Kane with a video call a couple of weeks earlier in June and assured him that their security and intelligence services had been briefed — ordered to lay off pursuing the Jamiesons on Australian turf or otherwise. He had called a truce and laid down the law.

Yet the American people had seen this as too little much too late, especially in the wake of the NASA revelations.

Calls for President Ashmore to resign became constant and universal. Eggs were thrown at his vehicles and commentary was of the most unkind and destructive variety. People called him a drone, a paedophile and a monster. His presidency had become untenable.

Ashmore's VP was just as hated — perhaps even more, responsible for much of the dark side of politics as he was seen to be. The crowds grew and grew until the streets were all blocked then Security abandoned the president and his team.

In the end, even the military abandoned the president and VP, the leading generals formally asking that they both step down in favour of the Speaker of the House, Buddy Carlsen, who was liked by everyone even if not everyone trusted him absolutely. The ultimatum came, appropriately, on the fourth of July and both Ashmore and his VP stepped down.

Buddy Carlson had been a news reporter in his early working years and had rebelled against the establishment in the wake of the new covid pandemic scare in 2035. He had established trust by opposing the government line and giving vent to the sorts of ideas that would promote freedom and human rights. Saying what virtually no other high-profile figure in the media would say at the time, he rapidly established a massive backing.

Now, in his forties, surprisingly young-looking and vital still, he had built another large following amongst

Republicans within the House of Representatives and pinched the plum role of Speaker from the weathered neo-con Ike Muller.

With the country in turmoil and the administration utterly besmirched by a number of dirty scandals and unpopular actions, it seemed that Buddy's Truth in Politics faction, born out of the crumbled remains of the MAGA movement had the only stable base.

Buddy's first action on being sworn in as President on July 5 was to defund the CIA, which he had sufficient support in Congress to do. When that was done, he called the Australian Prime Minister, Anthony Kane and asked for the private number of Alex Jamieson.

Wishing the contact to be through legitimate established and open channels, he did not ask for any secret information or shady avenues to establish contact with someone he respected and that he knew a great many of the American people also respected.

Thus, it was with some care and forethought that he called Jamieson on his own cell phone at eleven AM Australian time on Friday July the sixth, the day after he had been sworn in as President.

Alex picked up the phone when it rang and saw that it was an overseas caller, answering the call with a mental shrug.

'That Alex Jamieson?' said a voice that he instantly recognized.

'Sure is.'

'Bud Carlson here, mate. Just wanted you to know that we're doing everything we can to call off the dogs over here. I've even sacked the CIA.'

'That's good to know, Mr President. It should do a lot to help ... and congratulations on your timely appointment.'

'Shook me up a bit, I can tell you. Been a bunch of talk for a while now but nobody predicted this thing would go as far as it has.'

'I don't think even Cara and I had any idea it would go so far ... and here we are, just about to head into town for the release of the new series.'

'The Rings of Fate. Awesome title that. It'll be my spare time reading for a while.'

'You've read the Reign of the Dragon series?'

'To the last word. Gotta say it lays down the law in a pretty unique way.'

'Yes, there is some smart guidance. How did you sack the CIA, Mr President?'

'Bud, please. Got Congress to defund them. They're all out of work now. We sent in an alliance of various local police branches to secure all their premises and documents. They'll be held in a vault in Congress and will be well sifted over the next few months.'

'You'd be the one to know what to do with them.'

'And you. Journo too, aren't you?'

'Yes, it's in the blood, I think,' Alex replied.

'We've got a huge job on our hands, here.'

'Don't doubt that for a second.'

'The deep state was still rampant even in the Trump era, you know. He was a good man up to a point but he really had no idea who or what he could trust. Since then we buttoned down hard and formed discrete trust cliques to try and prevent infiltration.'

'Good idea. I don't know how you vet people for that but Thor treated it like a society of friends. If you weren't comfortable with someone for whatever reason, you just wouldn't let him in. But by the same token, you have to guard against becoming too insular.'

'Yes, it's always a fine line ... but I have to say ... those NASA files from Mars couldn't have found a better home. I've spoken to a Mike Carlsen from NASA quite a bit recently. We had him under protection after that nasty business at NASA HQ and he reckons the editing job was excellent.'

Alex laughed a little sourly.

'I won't make any admissions about all that just yet ... but you can be sure that if some creative licence and selective editing were best for the final outcome, we will have done it. It's way too important, Bud. We're none of us here all that long and we leave what we've done for others to enjoy or wade through. Don't much like wading through shit myself so I figured we'd do something for generations to come.'

'Yes, you're a man after my own heart ... and I wasn't trying to trap you with that ... just wanted you to know that either way, with respect to how it happened, I'm good with you guys and the result.'

'Thank you, Mr President. You know that it's not easy to get anything done. But this has the potential to supercharge the human race ... maybe for a generation or two, maybe even for a century or two and yes, it's damn good to be a part of it ... damn good for anyone who's a part of it.'

'Glad you see it that way and I do too ... but don't get too excited yet about what's going to happen in the short term. The deep state mess here in the US is just that ... deep and complicated. We're doing our best to unplug it and dig out the roots but from what I can make out, even if we cut off all known financial resources, it will still be able to survive on its own.'

'Take care doing that Bud. I hope you have a lot of good people around you on protection duty because you're going to need it.'

'True, my friend, and we're pretty thoughtful about how we employ these guys. But don't worry about us. Just you look after yourself and that lovely girl of yours. I hope this takes the pressure off for a little.'

'Off in one area, on in another, I think, for quite a while yet. We've got this book release for the Rings of Fate tomorrow and The Little River is doing another public meeting right after it ... in the same place.'

'The Domain, right? Cool name that. I hope it all goes well. The Little River, huh? I've heard a little about it. Maybe we could have something like that here. Sure got the raw material for it.'

'Yes, there will be a lot of good people out there looking for something to do now. Little Rivers turn into Big Rivers after all.'

Chapter 22 — Books and Bad Guys

If the last book release had been a good size and amply provided for, this one would be massive and unprovided for, food wise.

Even as they approached the area, it became obvious why Carmen Richards had chosen to fly them in by drone car. Drone car operation in the city was limited to hire operators and this one had been retained for the whole day.

Carmen new very well that the Little River meeting scheduled for later this Saturday afternoon would hold most of the crowd there. The launch was scheduled for one and the Little River meeting for four-thirty so the drone car would be needed to fly the great literary couple in, fly them out again for a late lunch then fly them back in again to attend the Little River meeting.

It was a strange sleek thing more like speedboat or jet than a helicopter and had eight electric motors driving fans that tilted through more than ninety degrees, half oriented downwards to aft and half oriented downwards and forward. Sophisticated sensors could predict short circuits or bearing malfunction hours ahead of failure and the controlling software instantly counteracted dangerous or unpredictable control inputs by the operator unless specifically negated with a red button in the middle of the stick — a button that had a firm actuation.

The interior was relatively stark but still comfortable and overall the feel was very space age. It was a fine and wind free day but the operator told them the wind did not make a lot of difference even when fairly strong. It would take a gale to make it uncomfortable.

Damon and his people knew that Cara and Alex were conducting their book launch on the same day and in the same place as their largest public meeting yet. They had undertaken to protect them and had provided a pavilion for their own use during the book launch and for Cara and Alex's during the meeting.

Alex had decided only the day before to do a little protecting of their own. He had set up the Compuscan to be carried in its special backpack with all the peripheral sensors and special aerials attached to arms, legs and midriff. When Cara saw it, she was immediately taken with its appearance and volunteered to be the carrier.

She chose a warm orange leather half coat and pale blue jeans and with all the gear on, she looked stunning. Alex had found out only recently that the device also had a range of sensors built in for detecting gases, radiation and all sorts of EM fields. Clearly, it was designed to be used in the field, at least in a pinch, and it had a crazy, beaten up grunge retro look about it that was in complete and effective contrast to the pretty blonde in her ultra modern semi-revealing attire.

Alex had planned to use the device during both events but mainly after their own, to listen in on service communications and give them good forewarning of any impending action by authorities. Cara would use it instead, now, and with a direct radio link to the Little

River people would be able to warn them of any impending trouble.

Sure, the Wolf Pack might have that sort of thing at their base but this compact version was quite new.

For the time being, once they got out of the drone car, Cara wore the backpack but had the headphones half off as she met people and shook hands with them. Many asked her what the gear was for but she just smiled and shook her finger.

Once they were up on the stage, the headphones remained half off but she still wore the gear. It seemed to suit her image but she also really got into monitoring the radio at the same time as engaging with people. The challenge of it excited her and seemed to trigger greater powers of engaging interaction.

For a while, she could not hear anything as the crowd's welcome cheering and clapping rose to a steady roar but after a minute or two it settled down and she lifted her hand, ready to speak.

'Hi everyone. It's great to see such a full house! I love a full house,' she said, starting her speech. 'We're here to entertain and inform so all the better that we can entertain and inform so many of you.'

Cheering for another minute.

'Thank you. Thank you. I know you're going to want to ask me about this weird kit I'm wearing. I just love it but really, I can't tell you. Just know that we've been up against some real dags ... you know in the real Aussie sense of shit clinging to wool, us being the wool.

I've had my flat broken into and Alex had his beloved old E-type blown up with a timer bomb.'

Loud groan from the audience.

'Don't worry folks, it's being restored as we speak and will soon return to pride of place in the garage.'

Loud cheering again.

'We've been visited and threatened by NASA scientists only to hear, flabbergasted, that their Head Office in DC imploded with jealous plots and counter plots resulting in a final act of horror in which dozens of people were killed.'

Some cheers and a good many groans of dismay from the audience.

'Yes, we were saddened to hear that. There are some good people there and we've even come to regard some of them as friends. Clearly this world is struggling under a deep burden of shit ... yes shit both organizational and human. I'd like to know what Thor and Odin would think of this foul mess because you'll all know from reading the Reign of the Dragon series that they struggled against huge odds on their own planet, Arya, to free themselves from the same sort of crapola.

'We know that the dirty elements in that world used the same sorts of attacks on their people. They laced their food with slow poisons, weaponized the health system to cripple people mentally and physically, they sabotaged the education system and social elements like literature, music and fashion to try to turn their people into sheep, ready for the slaughter. We know it. We've seen it and damn but we find out that it was all done on Arya twenty thousand years ago before the gods even became godlike with their powers and immortality!'

A hush of awe from the crowd.

'Yes, and who can know? Maybe that's what we face now. In the face of this challenge, will we execute the final victory and discover the true answers to our need for peace, prosperity and health ... bringing us effectively to the threshold of immortality? Do we experience these challenges so that we can bring ourselves within sight of that goal? I sure hope so. They say that evil always works against itself but maybe only if the good work for themselves.'

Massive cheering and clapping came on then and continued for a full three minutes.

'I'll hand you over to Alex now,' she continued as the applause dissipated, 'and he's going to talk to you about something we were discussing only last night. Stay well! Be happy.'

More uproarious cheering. Alex had to wait a while but eventually the crowd hushed again so that he could speak.

'You definitely have the right attitude!'

Another burst of cheering.

'She looks like a rock star, doesn't she?' said Alex into the mike and he looked almost angry as he said it.

Loud cheering drowned him out for a while.

'And you know, she can sing ... as well as play the piano and guitar. We're lucky to have her.'

Extended loud clapping.

'I'm guessing you've all read the Reign series. It's pretty straightforward and I'm not going to need to explain it all to you so I'm going to get to the nitty-gritty and just tell you how this new series is different to Reign. Yes, Cara and I were discussing it only last night because its message is a more subtle one and we both ended up wondering if it even had a specific message.'

The crowd now remained silent, expectant.

'Reign of the Dragon tells us quite directly how we should behave, what to do and how not to behave. It makes it really clear why we can't go easy on these arseholes. The Rings of Fate is very different and tells us a romantic tale of adventure, sorrow and triumph from our ancient past, here on Earth ... on Midgard. Well, Cara and I decided in the end that these books were a much greater gift then we first thought.

'There are so many things we can learn from them and they'll be a rich source every time we dip into them, well into the future. It's like the first series was the motivation and the why but this next series about our ancient romantic past is the how ... the how of how we change the way we feel about ourselves.'

A sort of interrogatory hush came from the crowd.

'Yes, it does seem to be a paradox, doesn't it ... but let me tell you, the gods love paradoxes. And it seems they love to tell us stories about how we can do things ... important things. There's little direct advice in The Rings of Fate yet it tells us in passing what we really need to know. The truths are more basic, more emotional, than in

Reign of the Dragon and therefore actually more fundamental and more important.'

A sort of hum of affirmation came from the crowd, now even larger as more late comers joined it.

'Well, maybe not more. The two series are the intellectual and the emotional sides. They're the yin and the yang. They're fundamental conceptual dichotomies. So, this marvellous series of six stories from beyond the dim mists of time, from well before our currently known history, are like to ones we have known already, like those tales that came from the pen of the great master Tolkien but they differ in small but crucial ways for the authors knew what he did not.

'These tales speak of love, of loyalty of, of honour, beauty and fulfilment ... but they also speak of hope and deep confidence in the purposes of the divine ... of a sure rising beyond the mundanity and purposelessness of this age we're now experiencing. Their standpoint is hope and strength rather than meek acceptance of tragedy and pain in the face of devastatingly overwhelming odds. Strangely ... yes, very strangely, these tales are very much for our time!'

The crowd then burst into another round of cheering, whistling and clapping.

'Yes, our heroes in the Rings of Fate are equipped for the challenges they face, yes, they do come to the fight with deliberate, conscious intent and yes, they do use all the tools they have at their disposal, despite intense pressure from the greatest druid of their time to avoid what he sees as a grave existential risk. And yes, despite all the great challenges and the tragedy ...'

There Alex paused.

'No, dammit, I can't give it all away,' he said then with a quick, refusing shake of the head.

Another brief pause.

'I'd be the last to want to spoil the experience of these marvellous books for you. So, for now, my friends, just read like there's no tomorrow ... and enjoy, knowing full well that there will be a wonderful new tomorrow.'

Carmen Richards spoke then for a while and filled the crowd in on some of the recent events of interest that had featured in the Jamiesons' lives.

Then Alex understood why she had decided to speak after them. Despite the fact that no one wanted the stories to be spoiled by his giving away too much information, they had yet been disappointed by not hearing more. He regarded these anecdotes of Carmen's, including their visit to the PM and his conversation with the new US president, as being crumbs given to satisfy the audience in the wake of disappointment — but the audience by no means took them as crumbs and in fact made a full, satisfying meal of them.

She also reminded the crowd that this was in a way a dual event, with the organizers of the increasingly popular Little River scheduled to appear and talk in less than a couple of hours.

It was a pleasant, sunny afternoon, especially for June, and the crowd remained to picnic, enjoy some new music, especially from the new rampant singer Aravella, to dance, to play and to talk amongst themselves about all that they had heard.

Some of the Little River people were already in the pavilion to host the entertainers, like Aravella, and Cara did the rounds meeting them with Alex towed around in her wake, smiling and having an absolute ball without feeling any pressure to perform.

After about half an hour, Carmen whisked them away in the drone car and took them to a little known but excellent Thai restaurant on Dee-Why Beach to indulge Cara's taste.

When they returned, the crowd seemed to have grown a bit rather than diminished and there was barely any space for the drone to land — except for one large bare patch of grass that the River people had cordoned off. The time was clicking over to near four when the Little River people were due to appear and it was growing quite cool.

There were two or three braziers in the pavilion and Cara did not feel the need to cover up while she wore the Compuscan backpack. She was comfortable and listened intently to the increasingly busy police bands.

Alex was outside with Cara's brother Brad and sister in law, Felicity, and they were looking increasingly intently at the bare patch of grass, which seemed in some strange way obscured and inert.

'What are they keeping it for ... a buffer zone?' Brad asked.

'I haven't heard but I guess that's always a good idea with a large crowd. Seems strange, though, doesn't it?'

'Yes ... very still,' Felicity noted. 'There's a bit of a breeze now but nothing's blowing around in there.'

'You're right. There's a few dandelion heads in there and they're not moving at all.'

Then the music ceased and there were some fumbling noises through a mike. Alex and Cara came out to join them.

As they looked, a man appeared about ten metres above the turf — rising up as if standing on a hoist but the hoist platform was invisible.

'I thank you now for coming ...'

'It's Damon,' said Cara, delighted. 'How did he get up there, and what's holding him there?'

Damon continued talking, introducing the evening's primary speaker without giving a name — and then there was Wolf Ballantyne, rising up beside him. A wave of new applause, driven by surprise and delight rose up around them.

Wolf stood with his arms raised in the air for a minute, acknowledging the enthusiasm of the crowd but as he dropped them to his side in a single imperative motion, silence fell over the Domain area.

'This world has been taken over by a machine,' he began in a deep smooth voice that resonated around the field. 'It's not a thing of metal and wheels but a social structure that inhibits and defies the true nature of mankind.'

Speaking incognito, few knew who he was but Alex could see that no one cared that they did not know his name. It was clear he was a born leader, not of the kind that now ruled most of the countries of the world but of a type long lost to the world.

He was received both with admiration and joy. Speaking of the world's ills, he drew people into his fold swiftly and surely, telling them of the evils that had ruled for so long and of the good that could come with a kinder, happier and more far-sighted approach. In truth, Alex felt he was the current embodiment of the type of leader about which Thor had written so long ago.

Cara was simply in awe. In part she listened uncritically because she wanted to ride the wave of the moment but also because she was listening to other things — a range of transmissions coming through on the Compuscan — and it took a degree of concentration to make sense of them and form the disparate fragments into a coherent pattern.

As soon as she had, she realized that a government attack was being prepared as Wolf spoke and would very soon be set in motion.

She slipped back into the pavilion and went straight to the duty officer in control there.

'Sean, you've got to contact Damon and Wolf straight away,' she said. 'I just intercepted a series of police transmissions and they're going to attack.'

'Now or sometime later?' he asked.

'Imminent. Straight away.'

Sean spoke straight into the two way and knew that Wolf could hear him, even though he did not pause in his speech or movements.

'Imminent attack, Wolf. Radio transmissions on the police bands.'

'In other words,' Wolf continued with his speech to all before him, 'when we're past having fun, past judging everything on its own merits and past caring about all that we encounter, the machine has taken us. Although age really has nothing to do with it, we feel ourselves becoming old, in the sense of being weak and cast down when we succumb to it.'

In the background, somewhere over towards the harbour, the sound of thudding chopper blades grew louder. Wolf finished speaking and invited questions from the audience, still standing up in mid-air beside Damon softly lit by a distant spotlight.

Someone asked if they truly had the resources they needed to help them stand against evil and Wolf was just about to respond when he saw something hard and cruel in the sky — several streaks of fire racing towards them in the half light. No, there were actually six, as all could see when they were closer.

With great personal presence and astonishing calm, Wolf turned and raised up his right hand as if to block or ward away the evil presence.

Alex could not believe what he was seeing. Was this to be a pivotal moment in history — the end, perhaps, of the Little River and the Wolf Pack, dissolved forever by government arrogance and met only with some futile gesture of bravery?

Yet at the very last those fierce streaks of fire simply veered away, turning around one hundred and eighty degrees in wide outward arcs only to race back towards the distant black objects in the sky that had set them loose.

Great booms and flashes of red orange light flourished over the city gardens and the dark threat was no more. Those who had been paid to silence The Wolf Pack and its leaders were now the surprise victims of their own callous stupidity. They had stepped up to do evil and had paid the ultimate price, sending instead a clear message back to their masters. Those hidden tyrants would now have to acknowledge they were dealing with something far bigger than they had ever imagined.

A great commotion sprang up then across the sloping lawns of the Domain as thousands called out in delight, admiration, surprise and hope.

'Did you see that?' said Brad, shaking his head and racing around in erratic circles as if he knew not which way to turn. 'Did you see how he just waved those things away ... and they flew straight back to destroy the choppers?'

'I don't know what to say,' Alex replied, in astonished joy, himself. 'That has to be one of the most incredible things I've ever seen. I'd have said it was all pre-arranged illusion but for the fact that those choppers just went up in smoke.'

'No, that was no light show.'

'But who sent them? Who ordered this? If it was Tony, he's not the man I thought he was.'

'It couldn't have been him,' Alex told him. 'He doesn't have jurisdiction here ... not with the police. It'll be that rotten Carmichael.'

Brad shook his head in ongoing disbelief.

'No, but it was illegal. Attacking a peaceful group of people attending a legit public meeting ... whoever ordered this ... they're finished.'

'You're right. And so is Tony even if he didn't order it. He allowed this on his watch. The New South Wales administration would have to have given him some sort of heads up ... some sort of indication.'

'Yes, it can't go unpunished.'

'Nor will it,' said Alex. 'Not by the feds ... not by Tony ... you saw what happened to those choppers. The Wolf Pack won't pull any punches after this.'

Brad grabbed Alex by the arm.

'We'd better get out of here,' he said. 'People are still in shock, still stunned about what happened ... but there'll be chaos here any minute now.'

Chapter 23 — Mountain Chase

Alex and Cara had grown tired and even a little scared of city life, with all it's threats and complexities. They also knew that their being at Laughton's place put Grant and Genie and all the others they associated with in danger.

Early in the morning following the meeting, they made the decision. Leave Sydney again and head for the hills. They had fast, safe transport with the Koenigsegg and they had a different sort of security in the bush amongst their farmer and hunter friends.

Laughton met them as they came down for breakfast and saw the look in their eyes.

'You're heading back to the bush?'

'It was a close call yesterday, Grant. I don't know how he did it but that Wolf fellow simply turned back the vipers by raising his hand. But he can't be there all the time to protect us and the people in the mountains are united against outsiders they don't like.'

'Not including yourselves.'

Alex laughed.

'I'm not an outsider. I've been around that place one way or another almost all my life ... and they love Cara. You know, there's a house for sale next door to mine and one a little up the road. Maybe you should buy it and bring Genie down there too.'

'What about Brad and Felicity? She's got quite a few relatives too.'

'Felicity's people have a property in the Southern Highlands. They'll be alright ... if they choose to leave.'

'Brad called me this morning. Said more or less the same things as you. I'll come down and see you soon and take a look at those houses.'

'Don't leave it too long. Others will be starting to think the same way as me pretty soon. After last night, the government's finished.'

'It wasn't Tony.'

'Maybe not ... but his agents should have been onto the state government more closely. It was just a question of time before that creep Carmichael did something like that. And the reaction will come.'

'You're right. Cara's cousin, Taylor, had a close call a while back and the whole family's pretty tense. Baying for blood.'

'And they're not the only ones.'

Most of the trip down the M5 and on through the Monaro Highway was uneventful but several anonymous looking SUVs appeared in the rear-view screen a number of times. New tech on the Koenigsegg enabled radar detection discreetly so whenever something like that appeared, Alex hit the gas for a few kilometres and left it far behind. Technically, the K had a maximum possible speed of more then five hundred kilometres per hour but on these occasions, Alex only went to a max of three hundred. Any more and it would be almost impossible to react to anything unexpected in time.

Cara watched the speedo with subtle glances from time to time and he knew she was doing it but he also knew that she was a closet speed freak. She was probably wishing she could be the one at the wheel — given how she was impatiently awaiting delivery of her very own new crimson and gold Agera.

They stopped for lunch and food shopping in Canberra before turning onto the Bobeyan Road.

'I've seen you sprinting away from those cars. Do you think they are suspect?' she asked once they had reached the more remote Bobeyan Road.

'I don't know if I thought they were so much as felt it. Now I think they were.'

'Then what was that one behind that tree just then?'

'A car?'

'Yes, hiding well back behind some trees in that lane just before that last corner.'

'What ...?'

'Sort of car? I don't know but it looked fast. I'd step on it now, maybe.'

'I love that, junior, you're telling me to step on it ...but this ain't no freeway baby.'

'You love that, don't you?'

'What?'

'Talking hick. Soon as we head back into the country, you're talking hick, baby.'

'Gotta play the part, lady.'

'Well, I'd rather you play the part of Speedracer right now because I think that one's catching us and look, there's another just behind it.'

'So, they have a team, gorgeous, it doesn't change the road. This thing has the best advantage on a freeway.'

'But it does handle well, doesn't it?'

'Let's see.'

On a long sweeping rise up into higher country, Alex pushed the Agera as hard as he could, knowing that not so many roos would be around at this time of day. Birds were more of a nuisance but whenever he saw them on the road he gave a toot and they flew off in time.

A long sweeper ended in a series of tight bends not so ideal for the Agera but at least the camber was good and he was able to hold the distance between them up to a point. The car in pursuit looked like a Caddie, which was lighter but still well endowed in the power stakes. Through the tighter bends they made up quite a bit of ground. Down the next hill it was tight too and the hunters made up even more, now only one short straight back from them.

Cara looked at Alex nervously.

'What's on their minds, do you think?'

He seemed unconcerned.

'They were hiding, waiting for someone and they followed us when we came by. Chances are they won't want to talk.'

'Could be just someone wanting to race?'

'I don't think so, especially travelling together like that. Looks like a Ferrari behind it.'

'American and Italian? Like the Mafia?'

'I'm not slowing down.'

'Good.'

As they fell into silence, they came to a longish bit of a straight and Alex pushed harder, getting back what he had lost in the bends. Then came a long series of winding descents with tight corners and they were back on them. Alex heard a sharp crack followed by several more, and something pinged off the bodywork.

'They're shooting at us!' said Cara.

'Damn, why didn't I order the dirty tricks options?"

'What would you use now if you could?' she asked with a nervous grin.

'Oil slick, for sure. Then we'd see some fireworks.'

Cara laughed, her green eyes glittering.

'Fire in the hole?'

'Yes, the big, deep hole next to the road over that Armco barrier.'

'Get that plate number, love. I'll be billing them for paint damage.'

Another couple of shots whizzed by close and one hit the rear screen, deflecting off up into the sky. Damn, that glass was tough.

Again, they descended and this time it was long and smooth. Alex hit the floor hard and the Agera leapt away like a god on steroids. They could hear the tyres biting and the wind howling past them. Every corner, no matter how slight thrust them sideways in the seats and the Caddie was left for dead. But then came a tighter climb followed by a long windy descent and the bad guys were there again. Bullets came now with monotonous regularity but nothing gave way.

'Looks like this beast was built to take all sorts of punishment.'

'My Ineos could have taken it too ... but not the speed.'

'Could've just rammed them and pushed them over the side.'

'Sounds like fun. Next time, maybe.'

'I'm hoping there won't be a next time. Getting tired of this to tell you the truth.'

Then they were in through Shannon's Flat and the country road straightened again. The pursuit was about even through there but when they reached the highway and turned left, the game was on for the Koenigsegg. They pulled away farther and farther until they were out of practical range.

The long straights and sweeping bends of the highway were perfect for the Agera and it lapped up the miles.

'Make a good racetrack, this road,' said Alex.

'This and most of the other roads around here. What about the Elliot Way?'

'Yeah great racetrack that one ... for anyone on a suicide mission. Ever stopped and looked over the edge of that on the steep parts?'

'Not really but yes, I know it's a long way down. Thank god we're not there now.'

Then there was the turn onto Middlingbank Road and the enemy behind gradually grew closer. It wasn't the tightest of roads but at the sorts of speeds they were doing, the Caddie did have a slight advantage.

Just as it came back into weapons range, Alex saw something ahead that sent his heart into his mouth. A roadblock — but as he grew closer, he saw that it was the locals, the farmers and hunters of the region. It seemed they were putting their road blocks out a bit wider now and protecting a larger area.

But they would not recognize the Agera. He began to slow but then the two large utes blocking the road pulled off to the side and he swept through, pulling up just behind a clutter of utes and trucks.

'They must have seen your plates,' said Cara.

'Maybe,' Alex replied, turning the car to face the action, 'but I've also talked to Ben often enough about my dream car. Who else but us would lob into here with one of these?'

The farm utes moved back onto the road straight after he passed and the pursuers pulled up a little distance away. A hail of shots came then but it was answered by a storm. These farm boys and hunters were dead shots and some of them had heavy calibre weapons.

Yet it was too much. The Caddie and the Ferrari were being torn apart. The lads were good but not high powered enough to account for the rapid, explosive damage. Within a minute the two cars were wrecks and their drivers were doing their best to get away with their proverbial tails between their legs.

A posse of utes followed the two cars for a bit, slowed down and running on rims as they were, but eventually they pushed them off to the side. A dozen men stood on the backs of the utes with rifles aimed.

Eventually, the doors opened and two men got out of each car, hands raised.

Ben was there with his son, Jay, and they came back to see Alex when the four were cuffed and thrown onto the back of a ute.

'You must have damned good eyesight!' said Alex as he approached.

'Binoculars, mate. Standard issue now. Can't really be taking pot-shots at strangers without them. Besides, I know an Agera when I see one.'

'Where've you seen one before?'

'Car shows in Canberra. Where else?'

'You'll be up for a closer look, then.'

'For sure but we'd better not take our eyes off the ball now. There's been too many shady characters trying to get in today and we've got to get a shift ready for tonight. The missus should be here soon with the steaks and sausages.'

'When do you guys get any real work done?'

'First things first mate. You know the drill.'

'Sure. We'll look in tomorrow.'

Just as they turned away, there was a sort of rush of wind and a large object appeared in the air over the road.

'What the hell?' said Ben, lifting his rifle.

The aircraft, a sleek swept wing design like a mid sized strike bomber, sank vertically down onto the road on its landing gear.

'Don't be alarmed,' said a well-amplified voice. 'We're friends and we helped you take down those intruders.'

Ben and Jay lowered their rifles and the hatch opened. Two figures in battle suits emerged, one taller than the other.

'I saw you at the Little River public meeting,' said Alex, breathing a sigh of relief.

'Yes, we're with the River ... or something like that,' he said. 'My name's Sean. We're here to take these guys off your hands and interrogate them. We need all the data we can get on any unauthorized hit squads.'

'Hit squads?'

'All too many of them around now. They might be from the RED but we can't say yet. We'll get it from them though, and let you know.'

'What is that thing?' Jay asked, staring up at the now silent aircraft.

'You saw that performance last night up in Sydney?' said Sean, glancing at Jay but directing his question at Alex.

'Sure.'

'Our new weapon. One was parked on the lawn at the Domain, cloaked. That was where Damon and Wolf were standing while they were talking to you.'

It made sense. Alex and Cara glanced at each other, smiling, happy to know the secret now.

'And how did they get the missiles to turn around and target their own choppers?'

Sean laughed.

'The redirection came from onboard software. Can we take these guys?'

Ben nodded.

'Do what you want with 'em. Here, fellers, give these guys a hand and chuck those creeps on board.'

As they were being handled towards the flyer, Alex caught the whiff of regret from one of them and stood forward in his path. Everyone stopped.

'What did you think your were doing?' he asked the one he sensed an undercurrent of emotion in, a tall dark haired Frenchman with blue eyes.

'Don't know what you're talking about, mate. We're police under cover and you were going too fast.'

'My arse, you're cops. Where's you're ID?'

'Special division. We don't need to carry any.'

Alex growled with low guttural enmity.

'Not allowed to carry it more like it. You're RED and the PM's not behind you. You're all out on a limb now and getting cleaned up yourselves. Good thing too. The world's done with black ops, blind killing and irresponsible government.'

'You think?'

The fellow's attitude was insolent now.

'You'll see. You and all those others who just follow orders without thinking and being responsible for their actions have made people like me angry.'

'Whoa, feller, you're making me scared.'

Ben clobbered him in the head from behind and he dropped to the ground.

'Now look what you've done,' said Alex with a grin. 'Somebody's going to have to lift him in.'

Sean turned to him.

'By the way, Wolf told me he wants to come and see you guys.'

'Anytime. He knows where we are and I don't think the lads here will be trying to stop him if he's in one of these flyers.'

'They're doing a great job ... but I'd be happy if they wouldn't fire on us. Probably wouldn't do much damage but no one likes getting shot at.'

'No.'

When the four men were loaded on board and the hatch was shut, the flyer lifted off, surprisingly quietly and rose into the air, suddenly disappearing when it got up to about twenty metres.

Cara and Alex drove on then and came to the Cove about fifteen minutes later.

'Do you think those guys were the RED?' Cara asked as they started to get dinner ready.

'Hard to say. Too many people seem to bear a grudge nowadays. I don't think it was the Americans. They were supposed to call off their dogs ... but who knows, it could have been either.'

Chapter 24 — The Wolf Calls

The next few weeks were busy. Outside forces made numerous attempts to gain entry to the northern Snowy Mountains region but ever since the National Parks had been defunded and expunged from the Australian system of bureaucracy, many small cottages and homesteads had sprung up throughout the mountains, giving the region many more eyes and ears than it had ever had before.

Anthony Kane had done that and it was one of his main achievements — one of the reasons why he had held office for three terms. His edict had been to disband National Parks and have homesteaders look after the region themselves in a more natural way.

After the 2019 fires, which had destroyed ninety percent of the Snowy Mountains National Park, a region which nature had never intended to burn so intensely, a good many people had become disillusioned with its methods and restrictions. If the restrictions were unable to save the park, what were they for?

Kane had told people that they could acquire cheap land in the mountains in lots no bigger than five hectares if they were willing to live naturally without town power, water and sewage services. If they lived with nature and for nature, they could control the feral animals, keep the weeds down and manage the burning in a way that was not destructive.

Since that happened in the mid thirties, the region had grown in population and much of the bush was regenerating like the natural garden it was supposed to be. People understood that if they chose to live there, they had to do it in a certain way. Far more rehabilitation had come from it than damage.

Many once beautiful areas were now well on their way towards regenerating and the whole northern Snowies had become a model for healthy, sustainable living in New South Wales.

The disbanding of National Parks had been a stepping stone towards Kane's longer term plan of eliminating state governments — but now there were other concerns.

After Alex and Cara had spent a week at the Cove, Grant and Genie came down with Brad and Felicity and had a look over two houses that had recently come on the market. Both were out of the younger couple's price range without selling their current house in Sydney but Grant preferred the larger house, higher up the hill. So, when Felicity took a shine to the house next door to Alex's, Cara bought it for them.

Already well-to-do, her wealth had grown a hundred-fold just in the last few months. Sales of Reign of the Dragon exceeded anything else that had come before it and now The Rings of Fate looked sure to challenge even that.

So, the deal was done and within days, Brad and Felicity moved in. The sale of the other house took a little longer but Grant received permission to rent it until the sale went through.

One evening, a couple of weeks in, after another violent attempt by a group to force their way in had been repulsed, the family gathered together for dinner in the large lounge room of Brad and Felicity's house.

'You have to wonder at all these attempts,' said Grant easily with a glass of red in his hand. 'Are they all after you two, Alex, or are they just miffed that they haven't been able to get in?'

'Bit of both I think. There's certainly a big attraction to that sort of challenge. We seem to have become the next Everest. Lord knows what they want with us.'

'Most likely vengeance,' said Brad.

'For what?'

'For being successful.'

'You probably have a point. We're sort of moral target practise.'

'Thank god for our friends, here,' said Cara. 'I don't want to be target practise, moral or physical.'

'I suppose the Wolf Pack is out there helping.'

'When they're not too busy.'

'Actually, they don't seem to be doing all that much at the moment. News about them has gone quiet.'

Alex laughed as he stoked the fire.

'That won't be for long. They're probably just in a planning phase. I mean, you should have seen that flyer. It just appeared out of nowhere almost on top of us ... almost completely silent. God knows what energy source powers the thing because when it lifted off again, there was barely any noise.'

'Where would they get tech like that?'

'Valhalla. The true name of Zephyr, apparently, and the prime asset of a very old organization ... the Templars.'

'So, they weren't all wiped out back in thirteen-o-seven or whenever it was,' said Brad.

'Thankfully no, even after the last killings in thirteen fourteen.'

'What makes you think they were so good?' Felicity asked. 'I mean, why would the Vatican have wiped them out if they weren't bad?'

'The Vatican?' said Alex. 'Well, it really was, I guess. Evil incarnate. The people loved the Templars because they helped them. They didn't seem to have any great interest in doctrine or Catholic dogma but they gave help to people when they needed it ... free loans even.'

'Free?'

'Free of interest. It was a golden age for humanity and when it was over, after Phillip of France had killed so many of them, things changed in Europe, much for the worse. The average height of the men in Europe shrank several inches over the next hundred years.'

Felicity looked shocked.

'The Vatican was that bad?'

'If you take the trouble to read your history ... I mean the reliable guys like Gibbon. Catholic rule has too often been vicious, not to mention ignorant and designed to promote ignorance.'

'My family are Catholic,' she said, coldly.

Alex shrugged.

'That might be,' Grant observed, in the mood to be conciliatory, 'but they've had the good sense not to be practising ones for several generations.'

'That's true,' she replied, ceding the point, 'and to be honest, I don't know who'd be fool enough to accept all that rubbish now.'

'Things are changing,' said Alex. 'Just look at this Wolf Pack ... and The Little River ... not to mention our own local community, here. People are more interested now in helping each other out than they have been in a long time. They've suffered enough.'

'Hopefully,' said Grant. 'It'll be interesting to see what happens in the next few weeks.'

Little did the residents of quiet Eucumbene Cove know of it but events in the outside world progressed with alarming speed and ferocity.

The first they knew of it was on the third of August when over the roaring gusts of a westerly gale they heard the strange whooshing sound characteristic of the Wolf Pack flyers and one appeared on the large terrace down below the house.

Wolf himself emerged from the flyer moments later, and struggled to keep his feet a particularly fierce gust. Both Cara and Alex went down to meet him. Felicity and Brad were out riding at the time.

'You seem to have gone very quiet in recent times,' said Alex once the greetings were over and they were heading up towards the house.

'Appearances can be deceiving,' Wolf replied with a meaning filled glance. 'It took a while but the bastards finally got up the nerve to attack us full bore. State police and the RED.'

'What did they do?'

The three went inside and Alex led them straight to the fire. It was bitterly cold outside.

'Bombed our most secure safe house. Damon's pad on Scotland Island. Early in the morning.'

'Anyone hurt?'

'No. It was a strangely pathetic attempt on their part but there were simultaneous raids on members' houses all over the state. It failed in every respect, of course. They're finished now ... gone for good. Surprised you didn't see some action here.'

'We've got the locals. They're a tight bunch and accustomed to working together. Glad to hear the RED's gone now though. Bunch of arseholes.'

'I know, Sean told me about that guy Keefer your feller clobbered. They get my goat too and there's still a lot of those sorts of people to clean up. To keep things ship shape, we've relocated to my place just over the hill. That's our base for now.'

'Over the hill?

'West side of the lake. Turnoff's a bit before Gang Gang Creek. Nice little spread overlooking the lake ... when it's nearer full.'

Alex nodded.

'Often wondered what was in there.'

278

'Well, now you can find out. We want you to join us there.'

'We're safe enough here.'

'Probably ... but that's not the issue. I need our best people working closely together now. There's a lot to be done.'

'But we're financial contributors ... not activists.'

'Not any more. That's all going to change ... pretty much as of now. You might not have heard much yet about what's going on in the cities.'

'Noticed the radio and TV were down. Internet's out too.'

'We did that. Everything's shut down now ... we've hit the system pretty hard already but I'm aiming to smash it completely.'

Alex looked shocked.

'Thought we were funding a struggling little rebel group,' he said.

'Like I said, it's all changed. Valhalla's big ... in ways ... and they've given us more of these flyers. Just one could take out a hundred targets a day but now we've got nine ... with more coming.'

'Then why do you need us?'

Wolf stretched back in his recliner, enjoying the warmth of the fire.

'It's not all hardware and action. Like I said, now is when we'll need our best minds. If all we did was blow stuff up there'd be no future for anyone. It's all got to be planned more carefully ... and you two have done more for us than you realize.'

Cara looked at her husband searchingly then back to Wolf.

'A lot of new agents wonder if they're up to it but the fact is, there are different duties. You might have an unspectacular role but it could be vital. If you think any action is only a small one and not that important, you might forget one little thing you're scheduled to do ... and it could be toast for everyone.'

'I see,' said Alex thoughtfully. 'So, you really are in this for the long haul.'

'Exactly ... and to my way of thinking, you were committed to action and didn't forget it ... even though it was in the middle of the night.'

Alex was surprised how good that made him feel. He had felt niggling doubts about himself for a long time and had begun to wonder if he was not just some soft, effete opportunist who had gotten lucky with stumbling upon Thor's remarkable tales. Maybe that was even true to an extent but now he knew there was another way he could commit. He had a need for a deeper expression of discipline and belonging but also knew he had the clear objectivity to help show the way.

Cara sat down on the lounge back away from the fire, having stood nearer to it for a while to warm up.

'So, now the fight's on,' she said.

'For good and all. The eternal war goes on. You've seen these flyers in action.'

'Yes.'

'But you haven't seen them at a tenth of their capability. They're quick as hell, armed to the teeth and invisible.'

'How many now?'

'Nine to be exact ... with another batch of a dozen due to arrive next Tuesday or Wednesday. Apart from anything else, we'll need good people to be trained in their use and to supervise their operation. As far I'm concerned, a good vessel skipper isn't so much a warrior as a thinker. As machines, these things are easy to fly but definitely not toys and a hell of a lot of damage could be done with them in the wrong hands.'

Alex turned to Cara.

'What do you think?'

'It sounds like we've been given the call.'

Their eyes met and while the same warmth as ever was there, something else was as well.

'It's been damned nice sitting around here just writing and being with you ... and the family is safe as well ... but now there's work to do.'

Wolf grinned happily, his kind, brilliant blue eyes smiling.

'I'm glad you see it that way. I was kind of counting on you. If people like you can't be persuaded something has to be done ...'

Cara moved forward a little.

'Yes, I get it too. Alex and I were particularly impressed with the latest books ... The Rings of Fate books. The Archer people in them suffered badly from raids and abductions but they didn't just leave it to the bigger people to protect them. After all, they were hard pressed too ... so they answered the call ... at least some of them did. And now we can do the same.'

'History repeating itself?'

'Maybe it is.'

She smiled.

'But just as war is eternal ... so is magic ... and we might well see the sort of world again wherein people use magic ... rings or whatever to build a better ... a better something.'

'Bravo!'

'Seria told us not long ago that those magic rings might even still exist somewhere in the world.'

Wolf stood away from the fire and again laid admiring eyes on her, seeing the love and wisdom beneath her gorgeous creamy skinned exterior.

'Well, we won't know what's possible unless we try it, will we?'

Alex nodded.

'It is a mystery,' he said, stretching out comfortably. 'Yet in those stories, when all was done and dusted, every last trace of the heroes was removed from the world.'

Wolf turned to him and shrugged.

'Who knows, brother, where it will all end ... and we do need to face the fact that things aren't always what they seem.

'In any case, I share the view of the world you both seem to have. In the last analysis, I'd rather not believe that the magic is all gone. After all, isn't that what makes life worth living?'

www.ingramcontent.com/pod-product-compliance
Lightning Source LLC
Chambersburg PA
CBHW050716180626
46814CB00002B/458